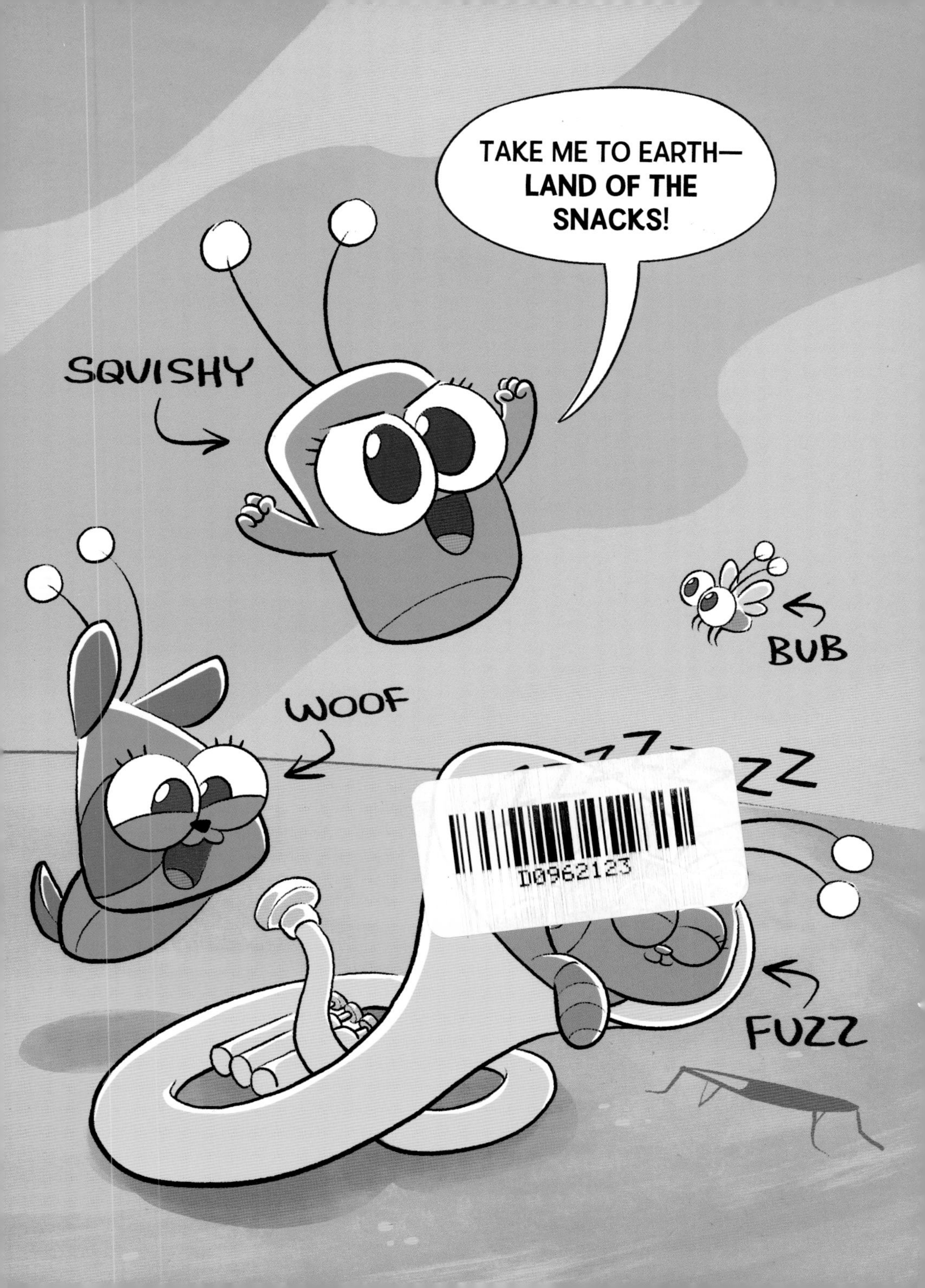
TAKE ME TO EARTH—
LAND OF THE
SNACKS!
SQUISHY
BUB
WOOF
FUZZ

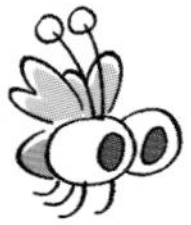

Want to read s'more?

Earth School

(Coming in summer 2023)

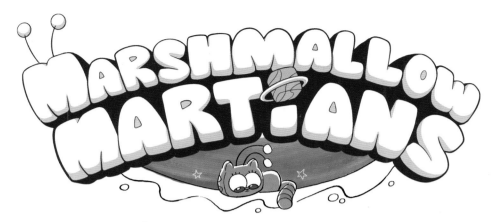

Marshmallow Martians

Show and Smell

Our first smell!

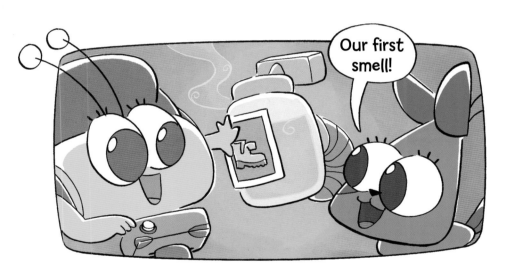

by Deanna Kent
illustrated by Neil Hooson

A STEPPING STONE BOOK™
Random House New York

This book, dear reader, is written especially for *you* with a wish
that it reminds you of how wacky and wonderful the world can be.
Please write your name here:

It is also for a few Earthlings called Sam, Max, Zach,
Jake, Jackson, Ethan, Ella, Colton, Anna, Charlie, Claire,
Mackenzie, Parker, Tanner, and Finn.
—D.K. and N.H.

Copyright © 2023 by GrumpyFish Creative Inc.
All rights reserved. Published in the United States by Random House Children's Books,
a division of Penguin Random House LLC, New York.
Random House and the colophon are registered trademarks and A Stepping Stone Book
and the colophon are trademarks of Penguin Random House LLC.
RH Graphic with the book design is a trademark of Penguin Random House LLC.
Visit us on the Web! rhcbooks.com
Educators and librarians, for a variety of teaching tools, visit us at RHTeachersLibrarians.com

Library of Congress Cataloging-in-Publication Data
Names: Kent, Deanna, author. | Hooson, Neil, illustrator.
Title: Show and smell / text, Deanna Kent ; illustrations, Neil Hooson.
Description: First edition. | New York : Random House Children's Books, [2023] | Series:
Marshmallow martians | Audience: Ages 3–7. |
Summary: Four curious Martians travel to an amusement park on Earth in search of the
smelliest smells to bring back to Planet Moop.
Identifiers: LCCN 2022004952 | ISBN 978-0-593-56607-7 (hardcover) |
ISBN 978-0-593-56608-4 (library binding) | ISBN 978-0-593-56609-1 (ebook)
Subjects: CYAC: Graphic novels. | Extraterrestrial beings—Fiction. | Odors—Fiction. |
LCGFT: Graphic novels.
Classification: LCC PZ7.7.K454 Sh 2023 | DDC 741.5/971—dc23/eng/20220506

MANUFACTURED IN CHINA
10 9 8 7 6 5 4 3 2 1
First Edition

Contents

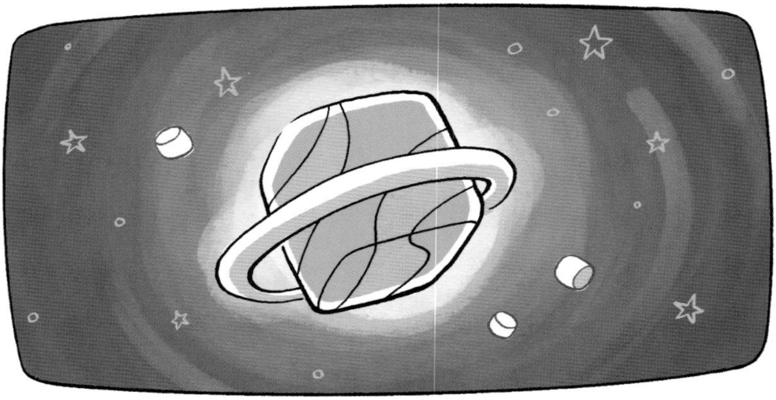

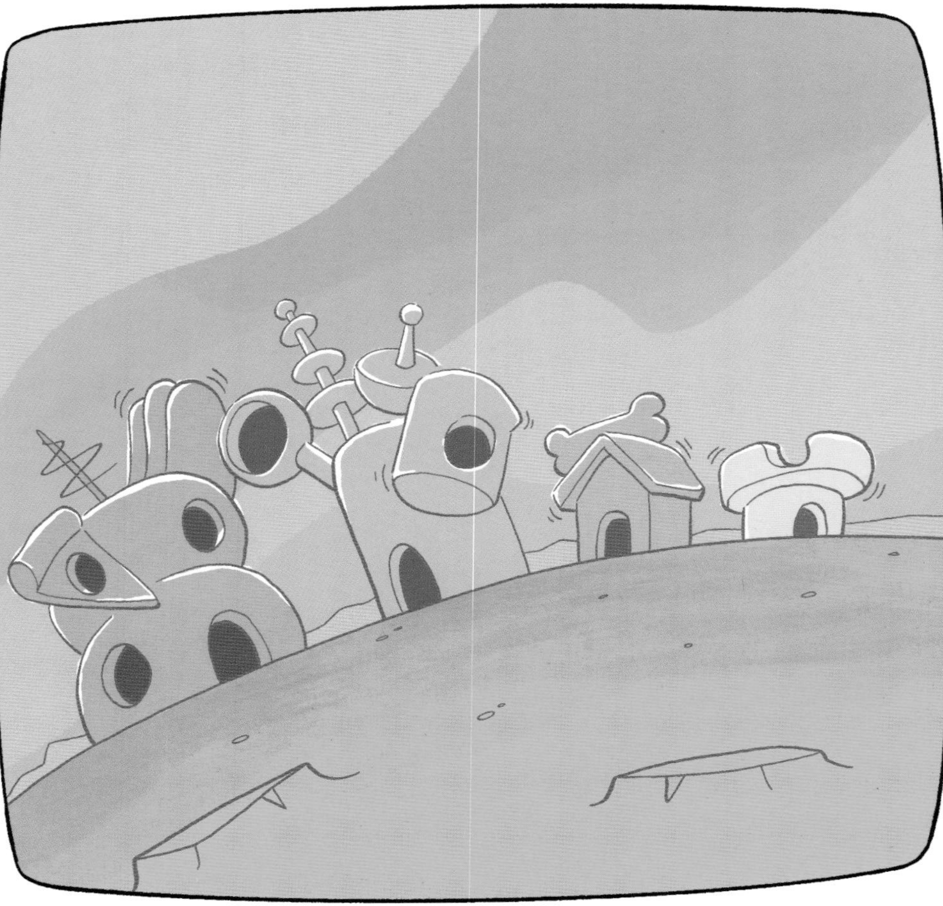

Chapter 1
Mystery Box!

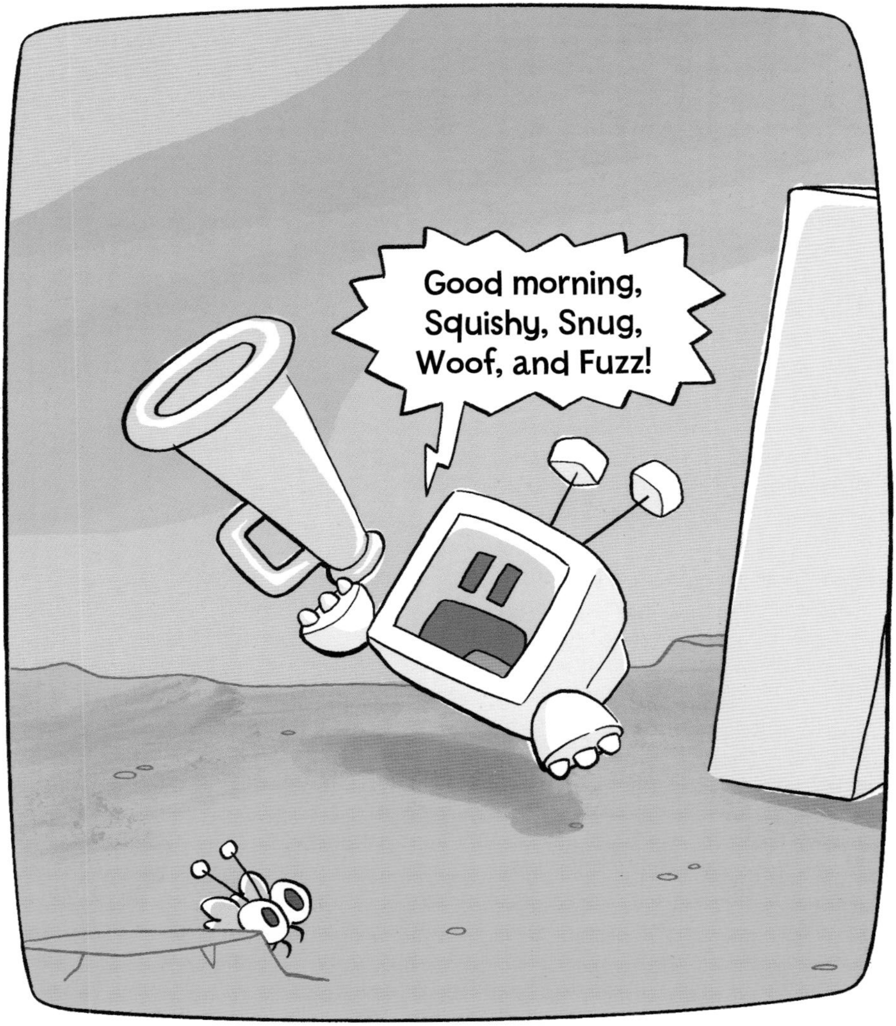
Good morning, Squishy, Snug, Woof, and Fuzz!

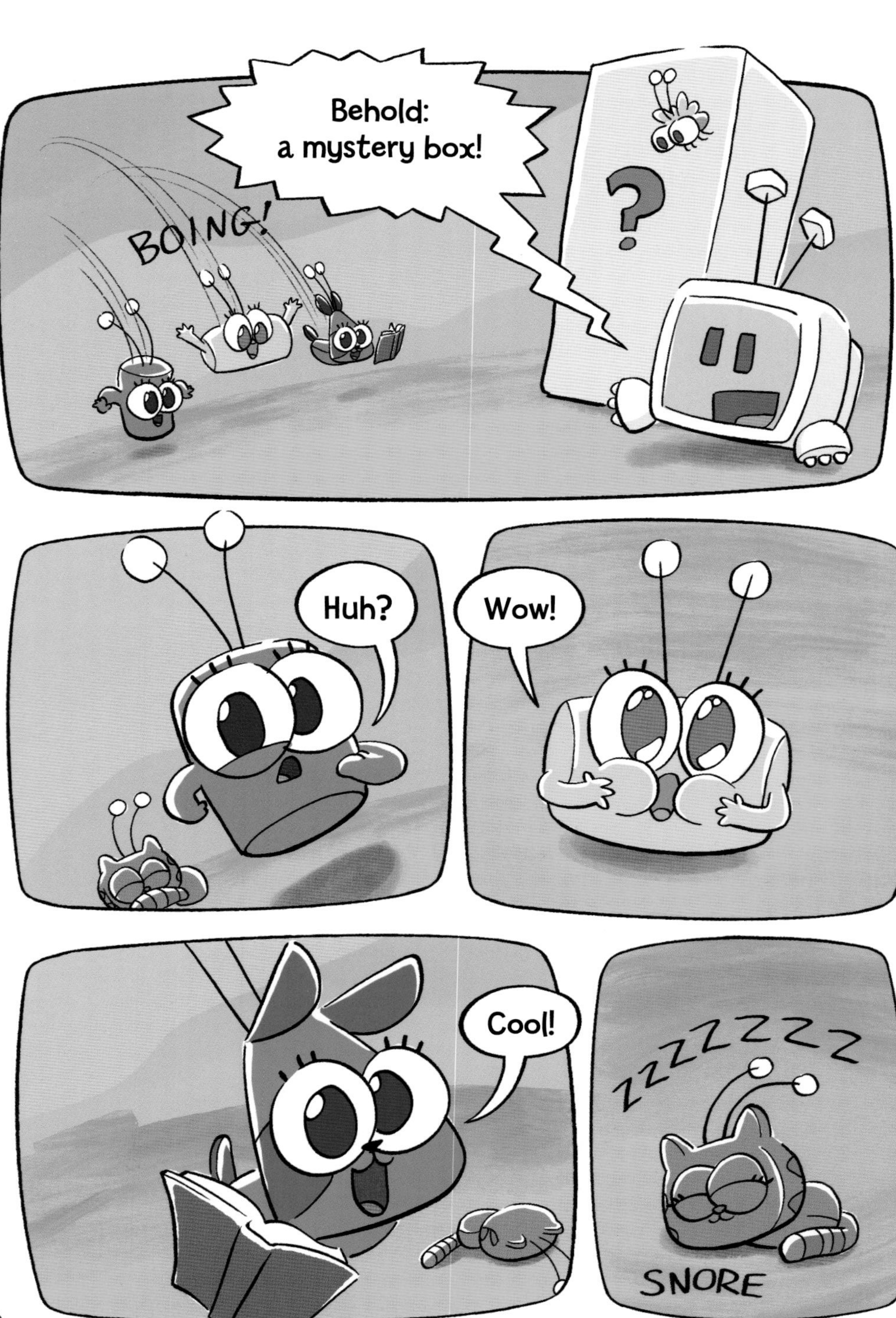
Behold: a mystery box!
BOING!
Huh?
Wow!
Cool!
ZZZZZZZZ
SNORE

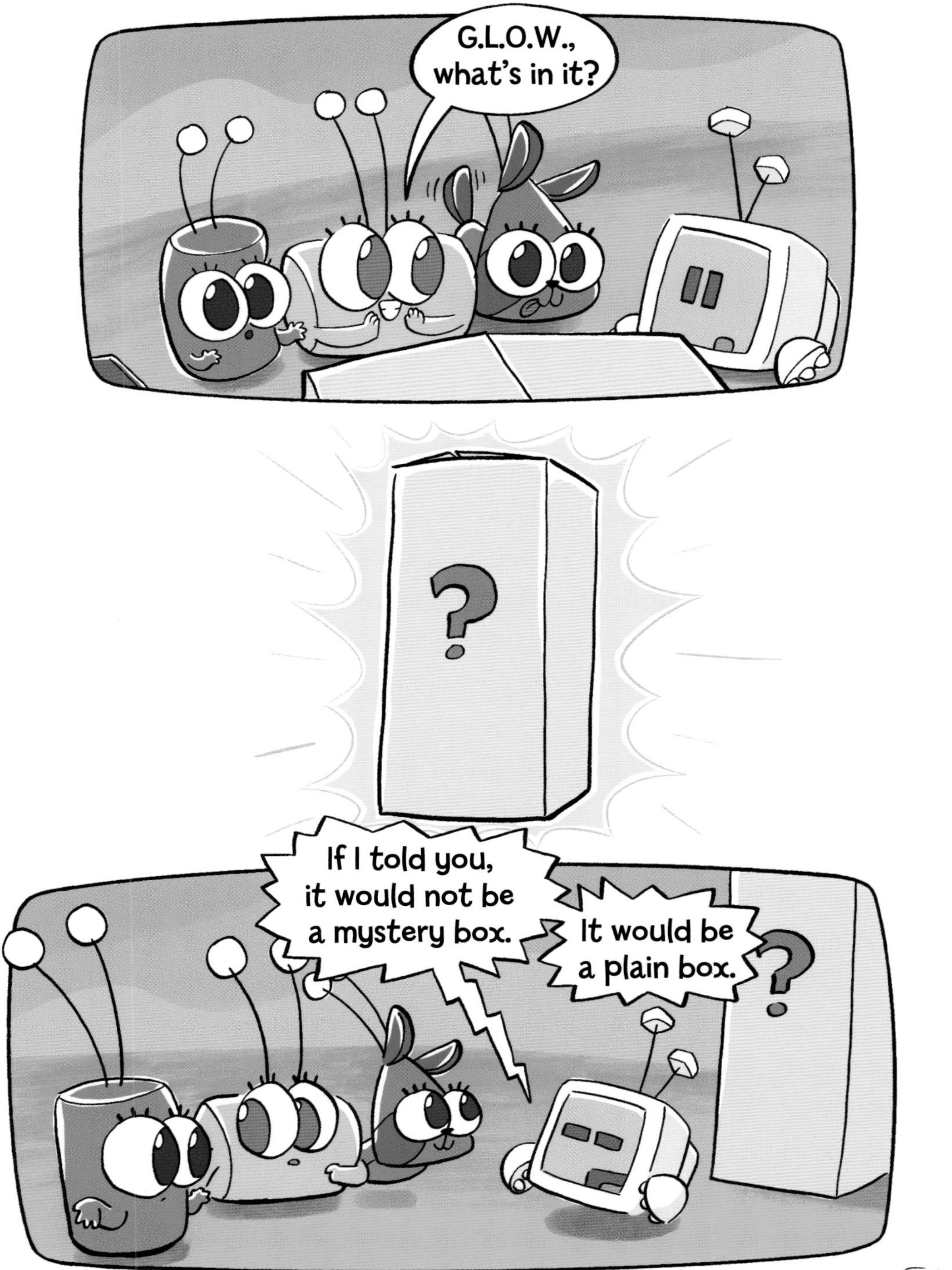
G.L.O.W., what's in it?
If I told you, it would not be a mystery box.
It would be a plain box.

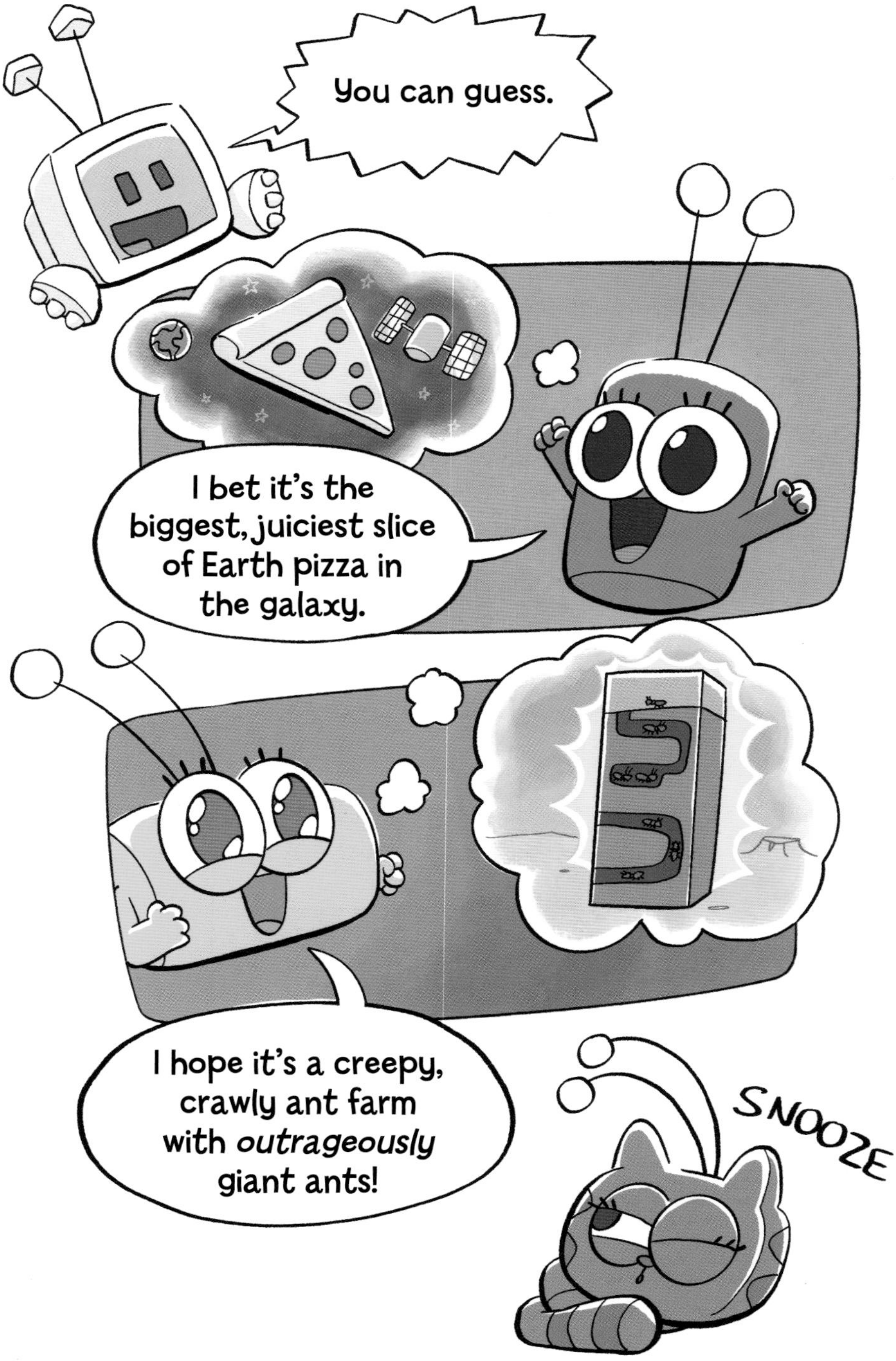
You can guess.
I bet it's the biggest, juiciest slice of Earth pizza in the galaxy.
I hope it's a creepy, crawly ant farm with *outrageously* giant ants!
SNOOZE

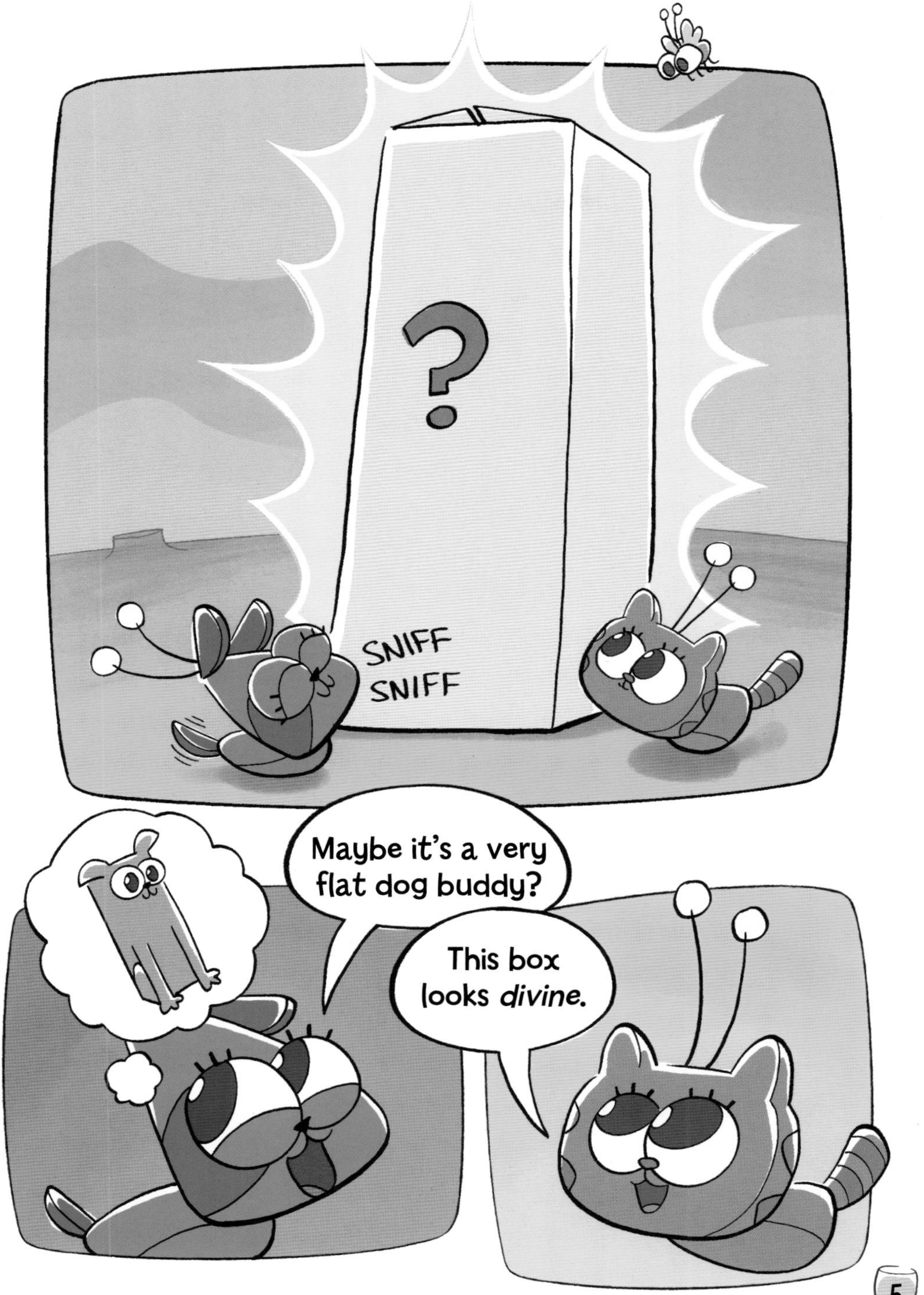

SNIFF
SNIFF
Maybe it's a very flat dog buddy?
This box looks *divine*.

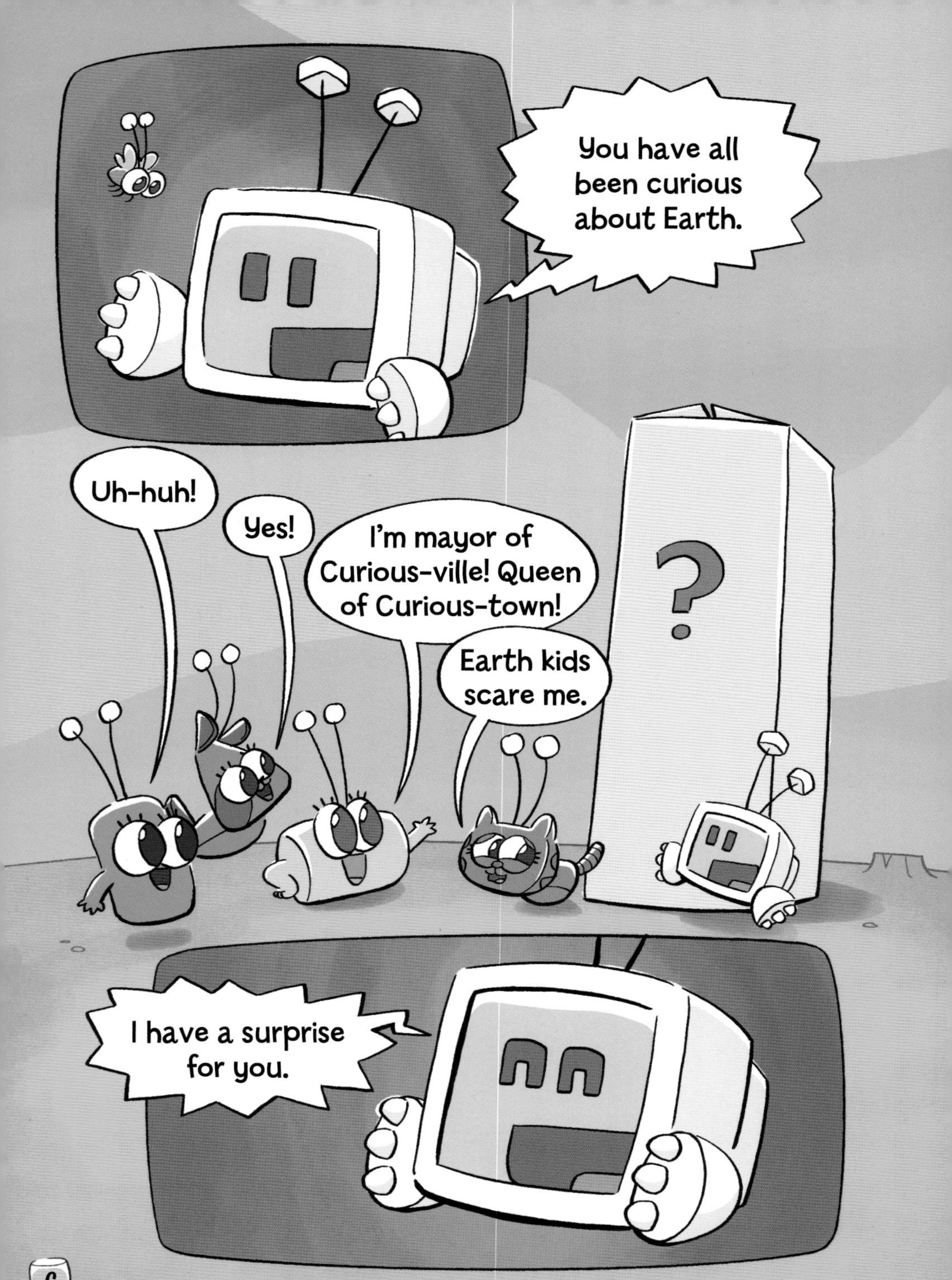
You have all been curious about Earth.
Uh-huh!
Yes!
I'm mayor of Curious-ville! Queen of Curious-town!
Earth kids scare me.
I have a surprise for you.

Chapter 2

P.E.E.P.!

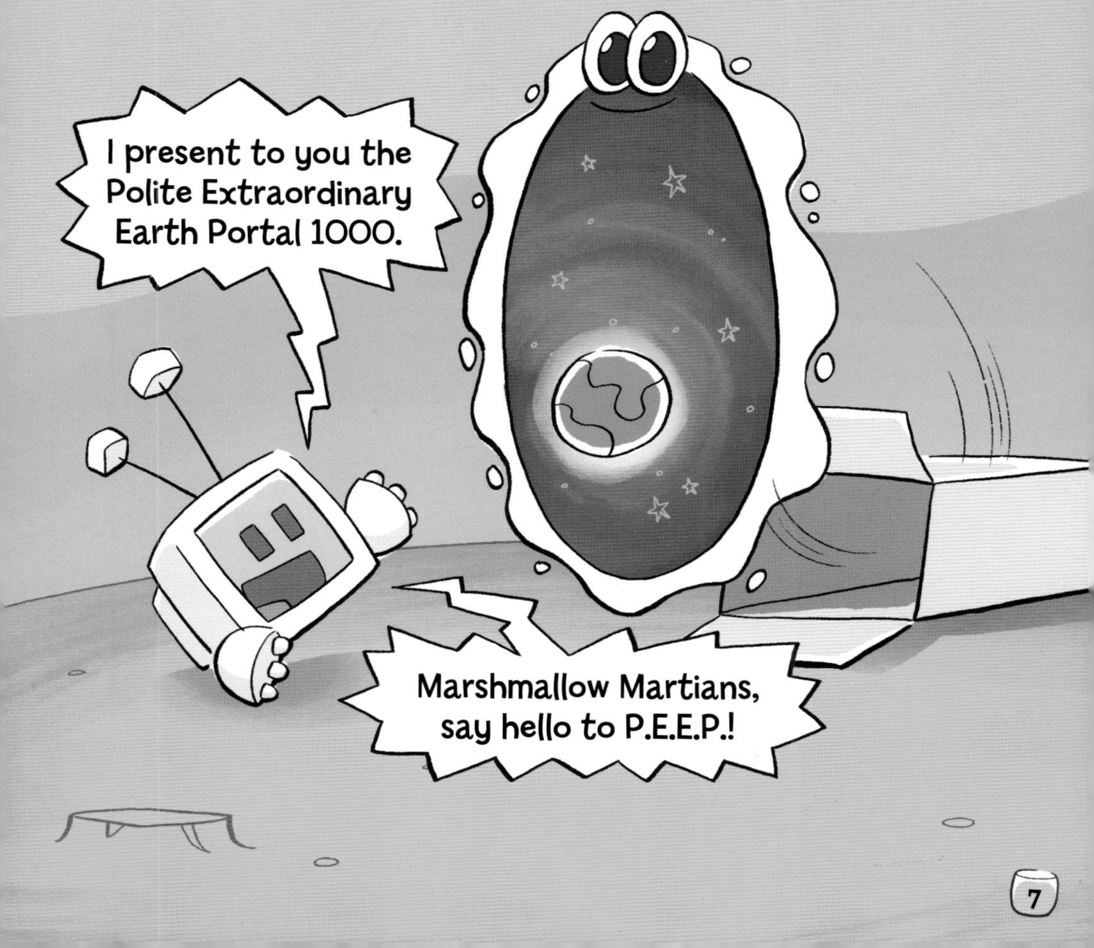
I present to you the Polite Extraordinary Earth Portal 1000.
Marshmallow Martians, say hello to P.E.E.P.!

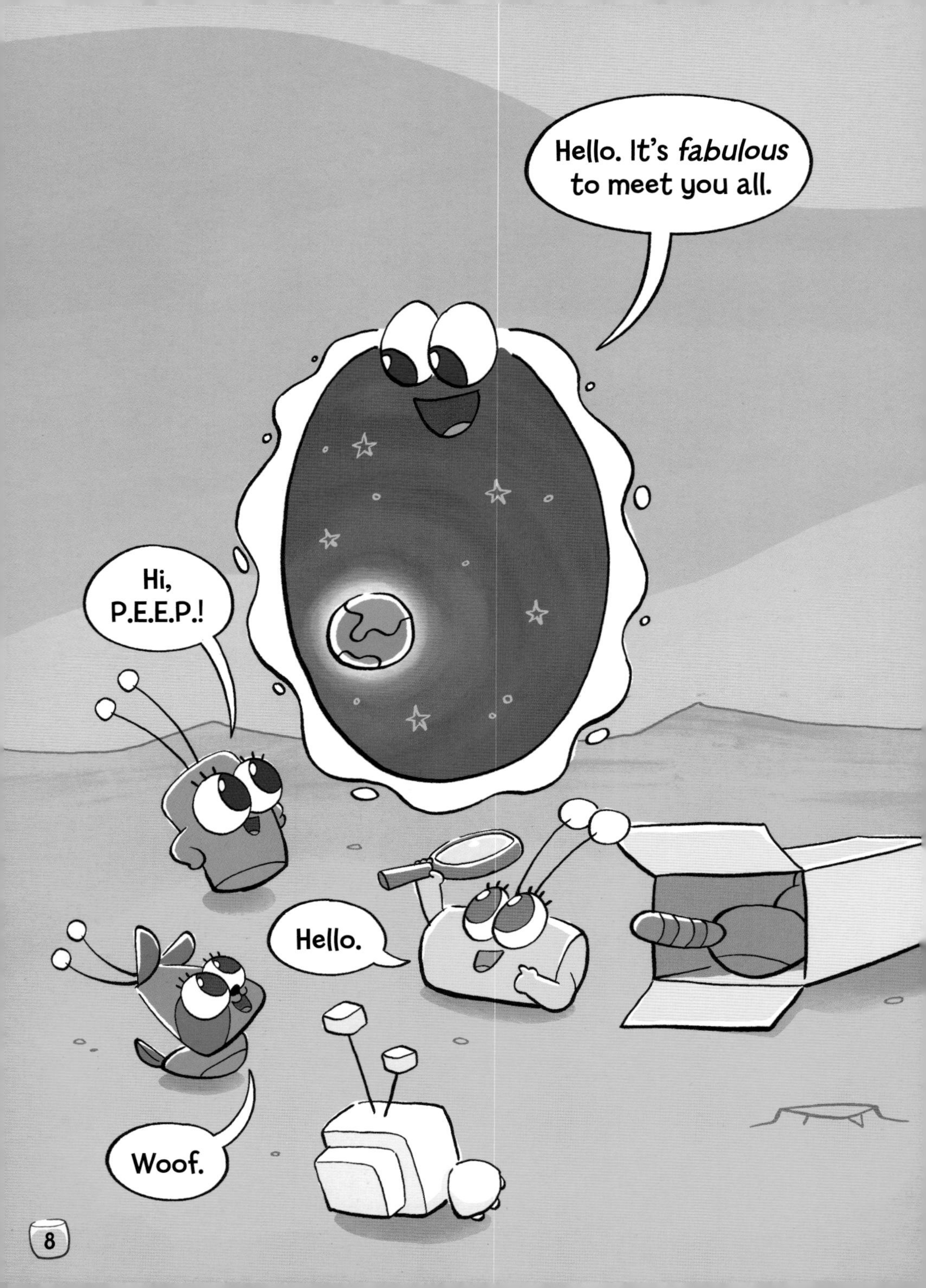
Hello. It's *fabulous* to meet you all.
Hi, P.E.E.P.!
Hello.
Woof.

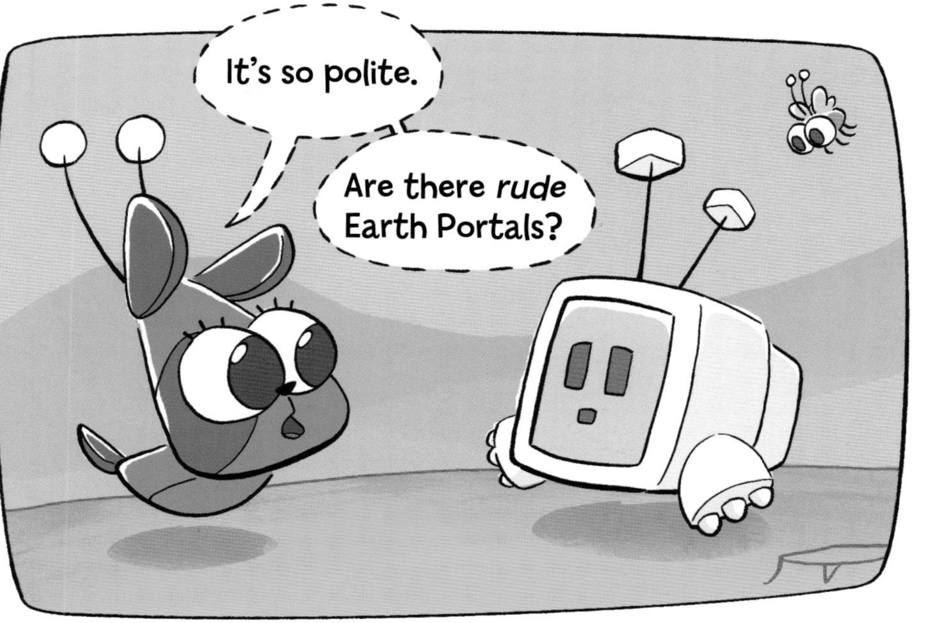
It's so polite.
Are there *rude* Earth Portals?

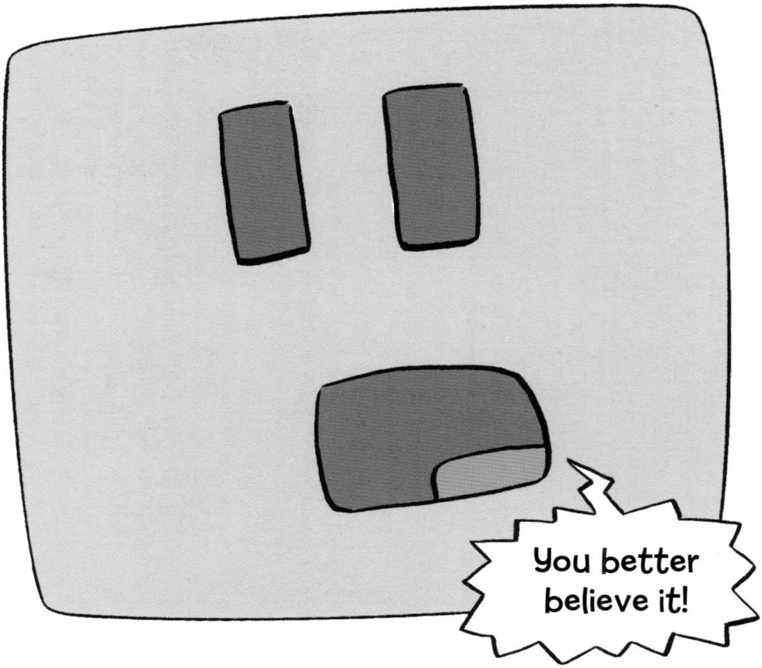
You better believe it!

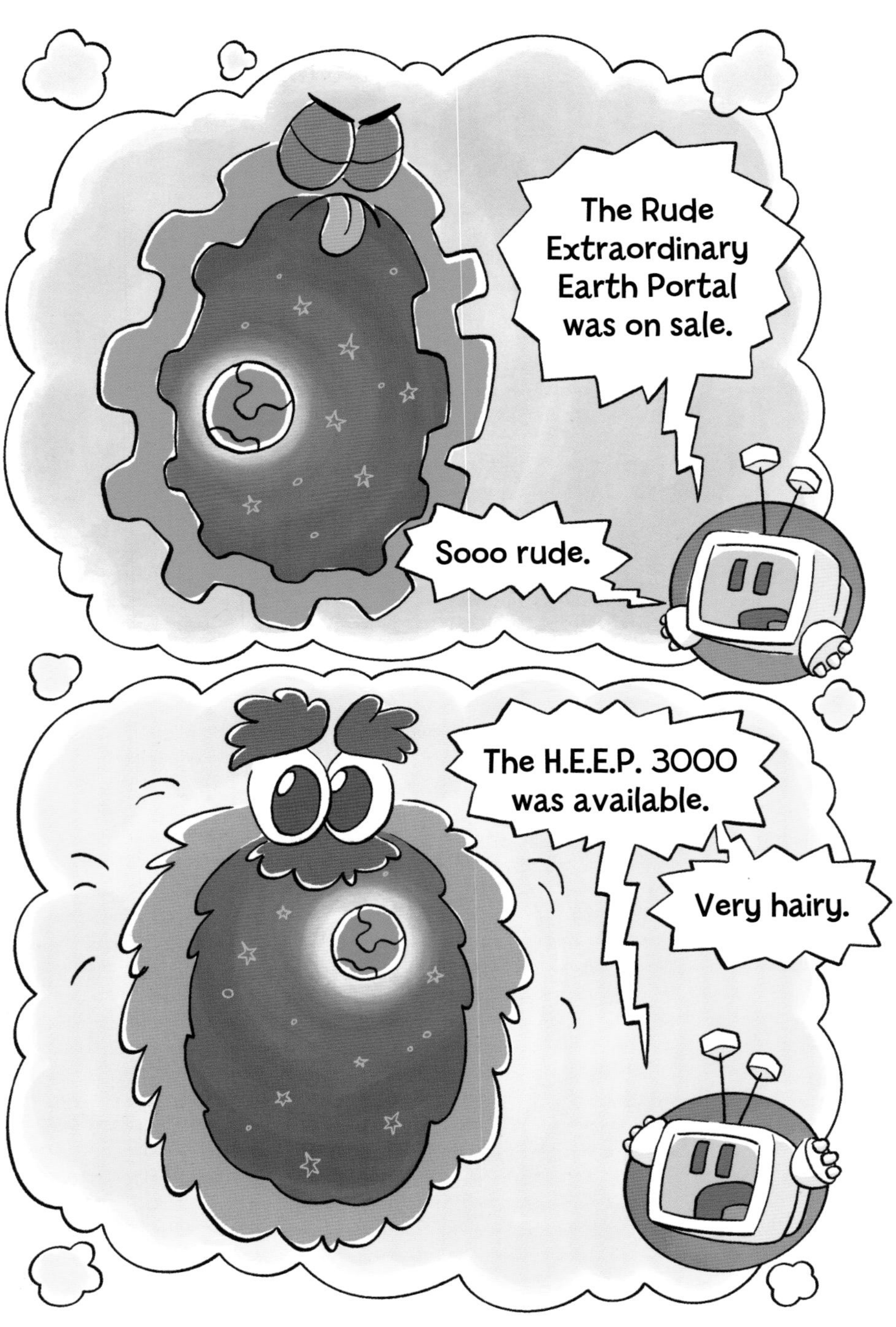
The Rude Extraordinary Earth Portal was on sale.
Sooo rude.
The H.E.E.P. 3000 was available.
Very hairy.

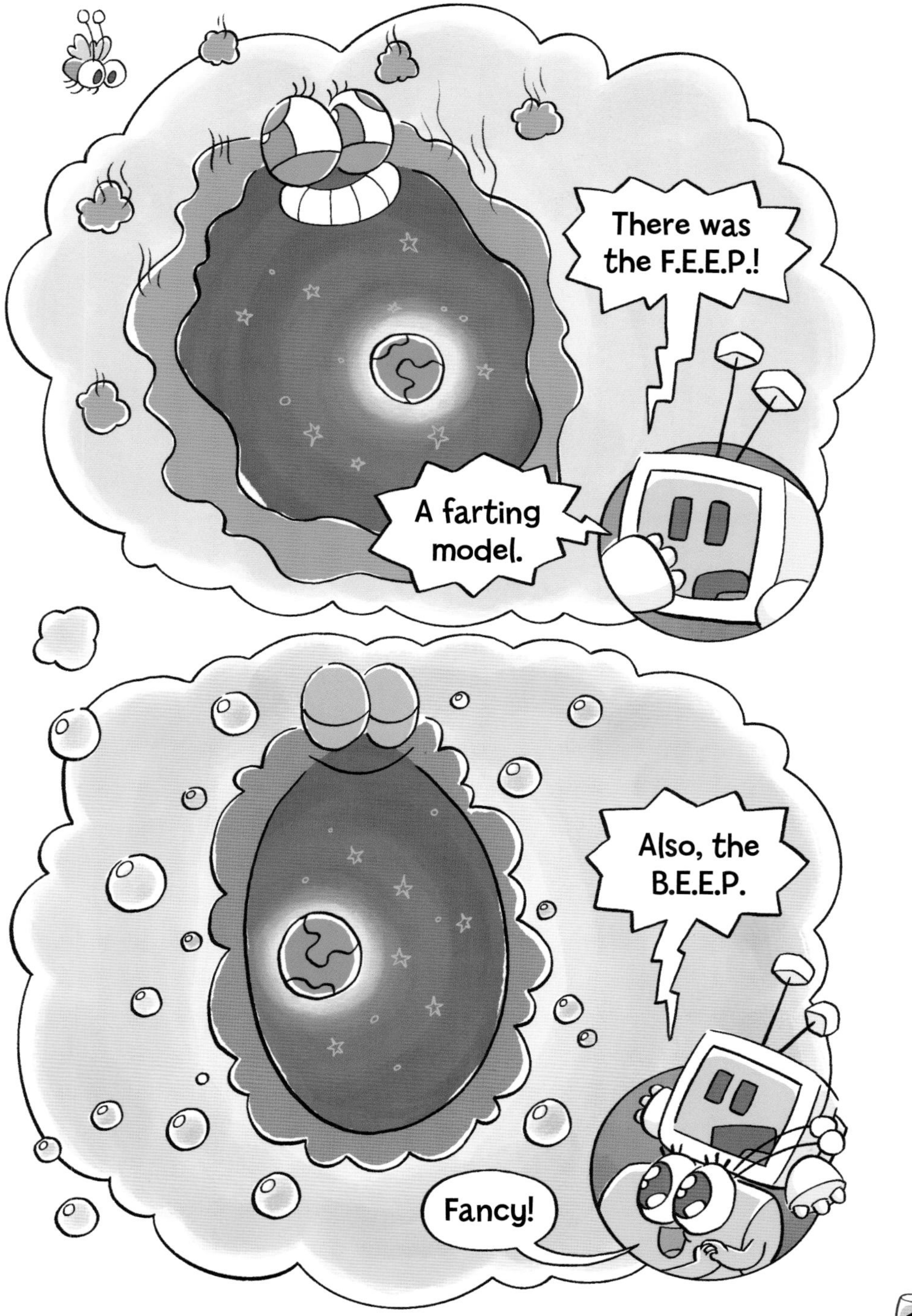
There was the F.E.E.P.!
A farting model.
Also, the B.E.E.P.
Fancy!

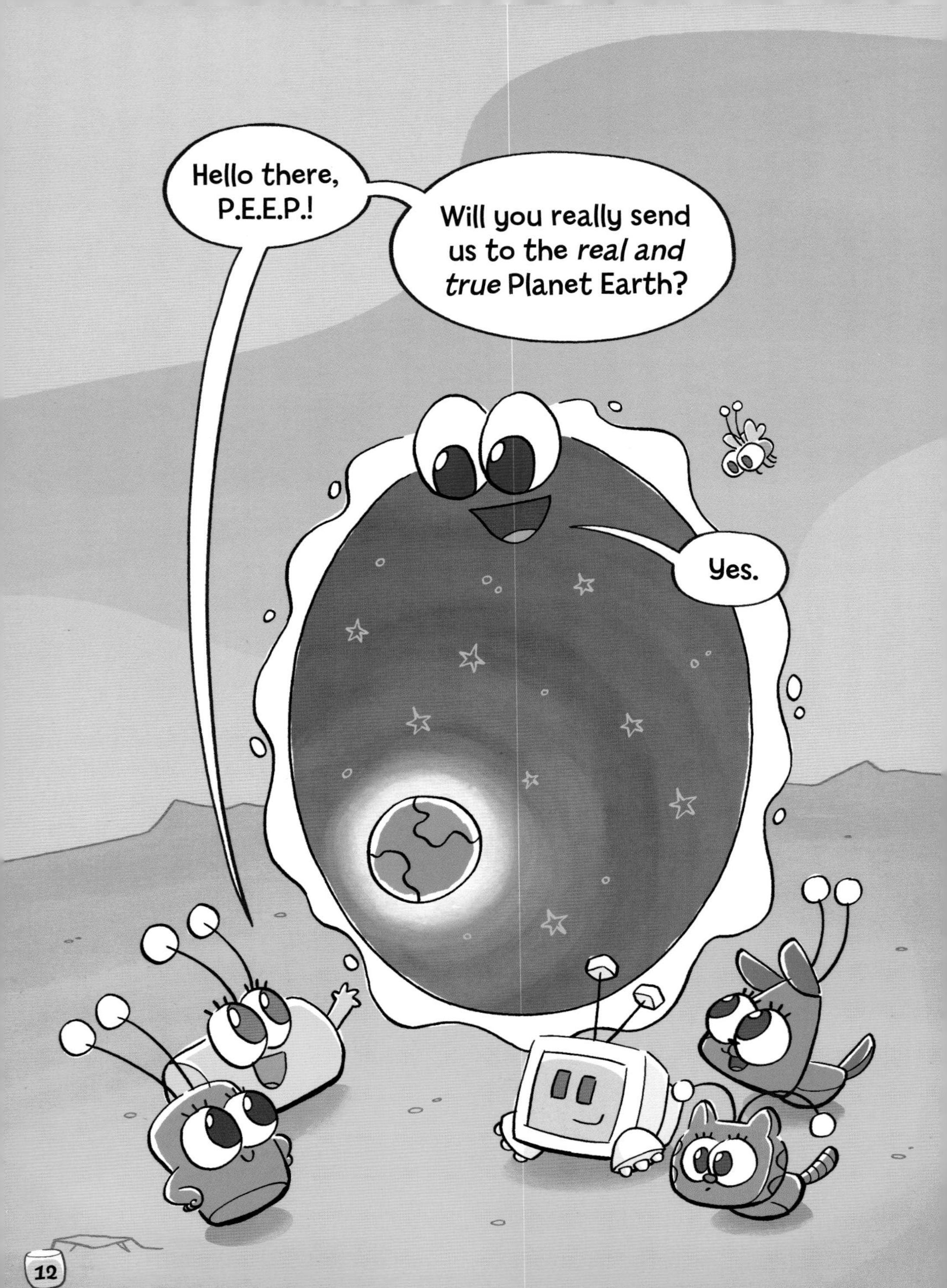
Hello there, P.E.E.P.!
Will you really send us to the *real and true* Planet Earth?
Yes.

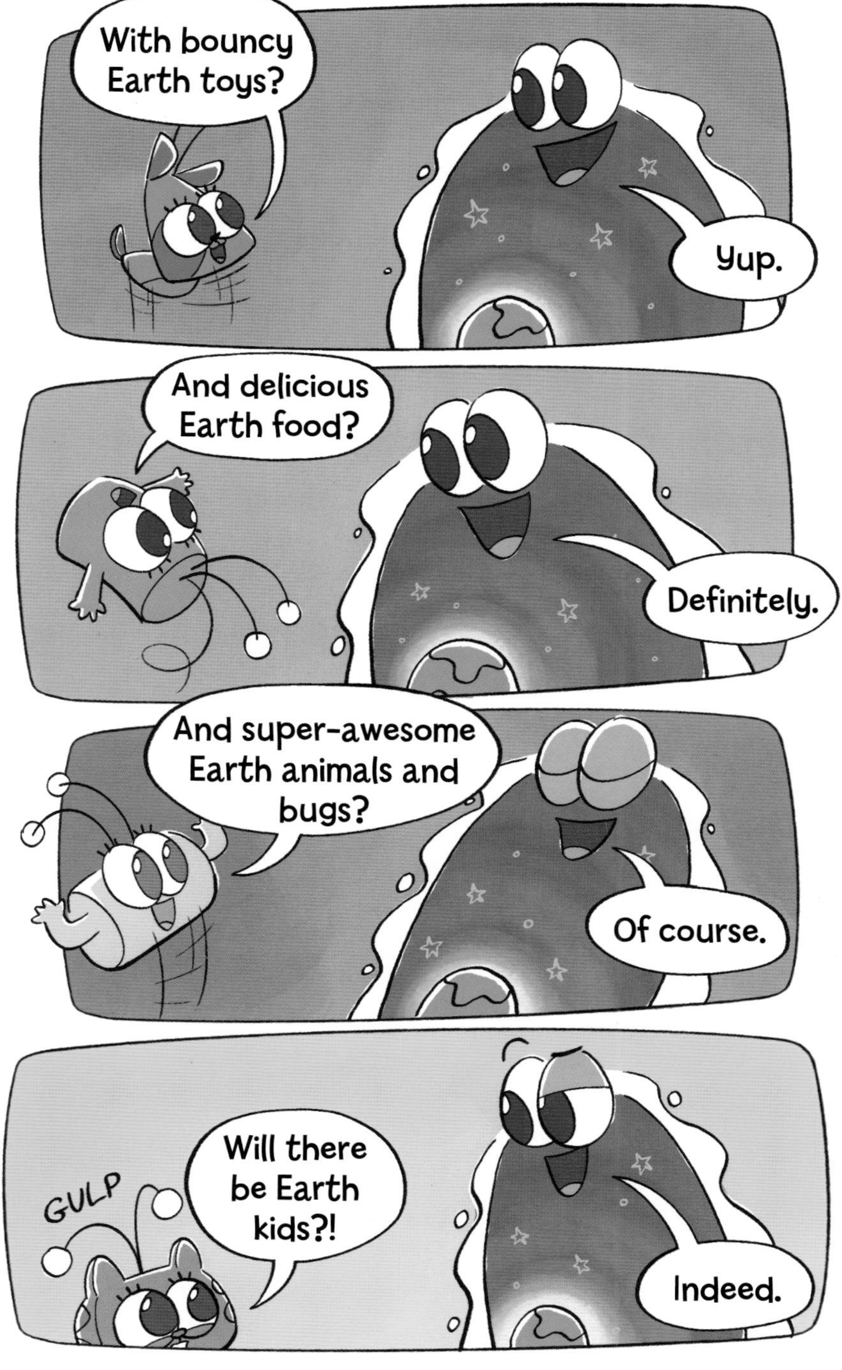
With bouncy Earth toys?
Yup.
And delicious Earth food?
Definitely.
And super-awesome Earth animals and bugs?
Of course.
GULP
Will there be Earth kids?!
Indeed.

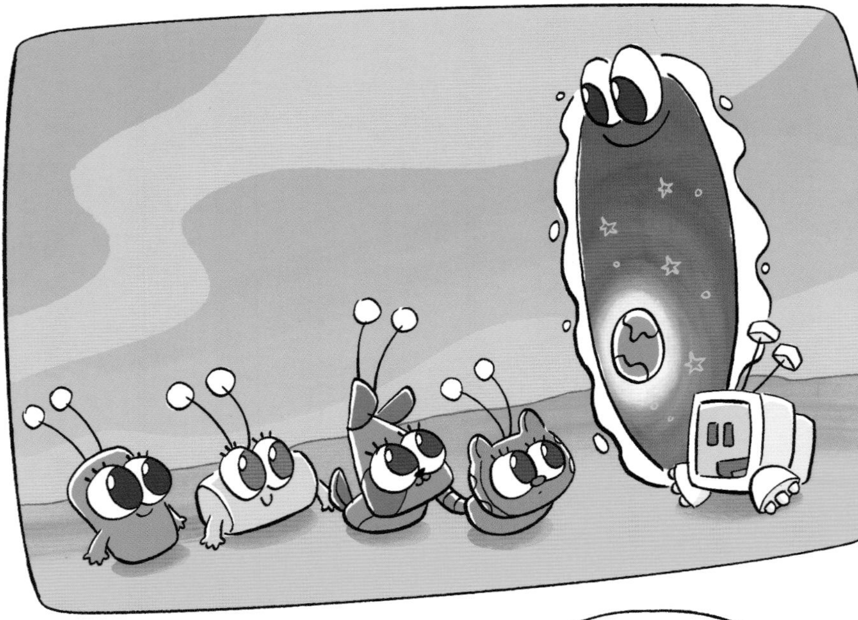

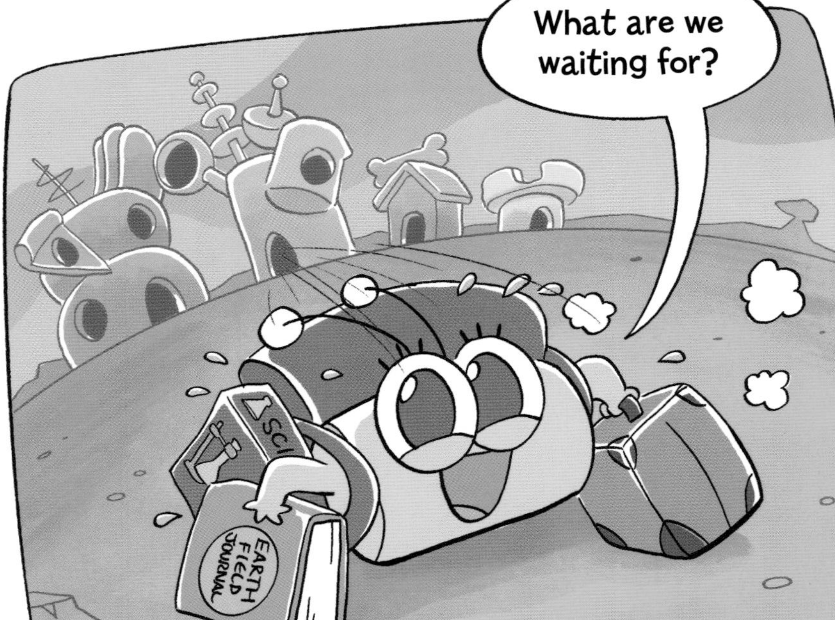
What are we waiting for?
SCI
EARTH FIELD JOURNAL

Chapter 3
Show and What?

LET'S GO!

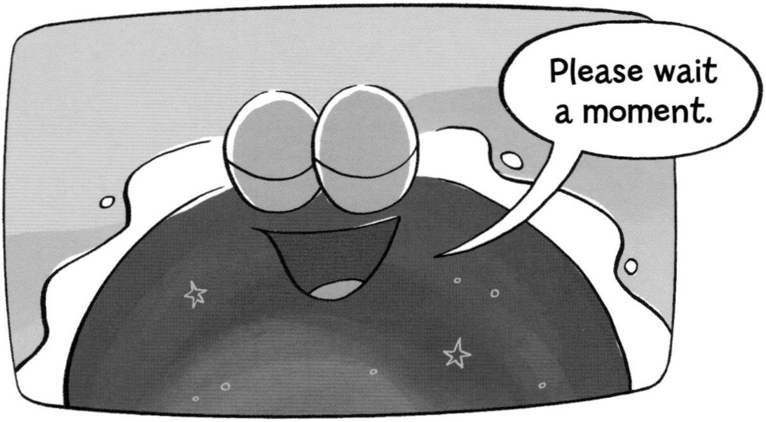
Please wait a moment.

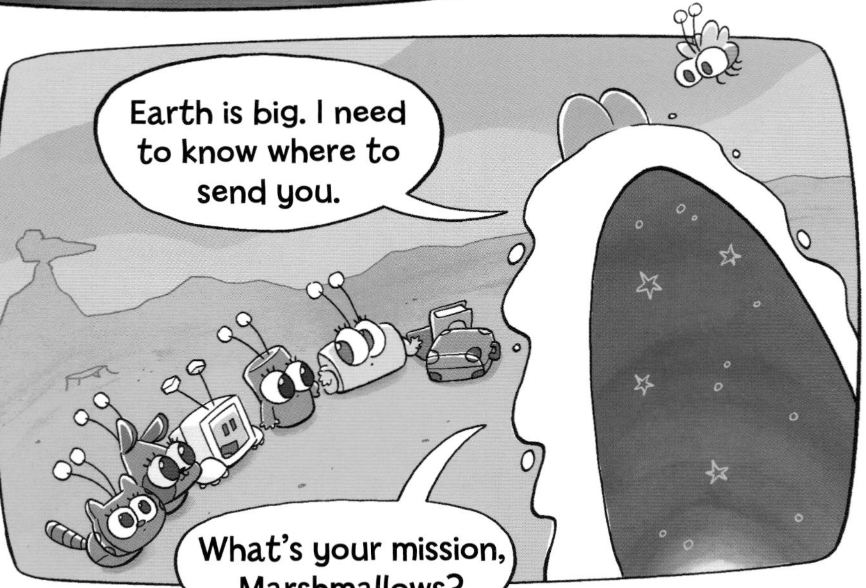
Earth is big. I need to know where to send you.
What's your mission, Marshmallows?

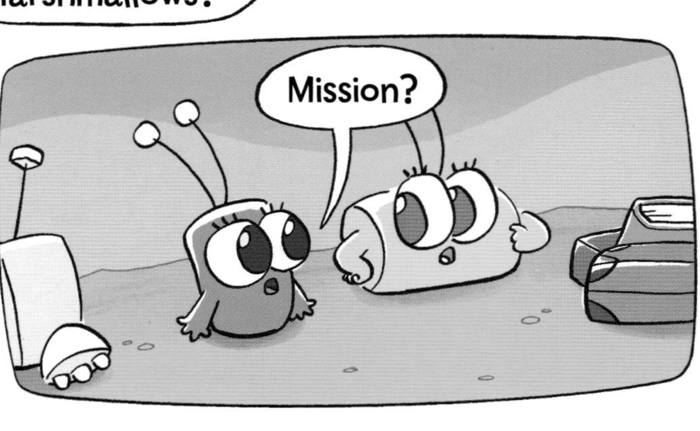
Mission?

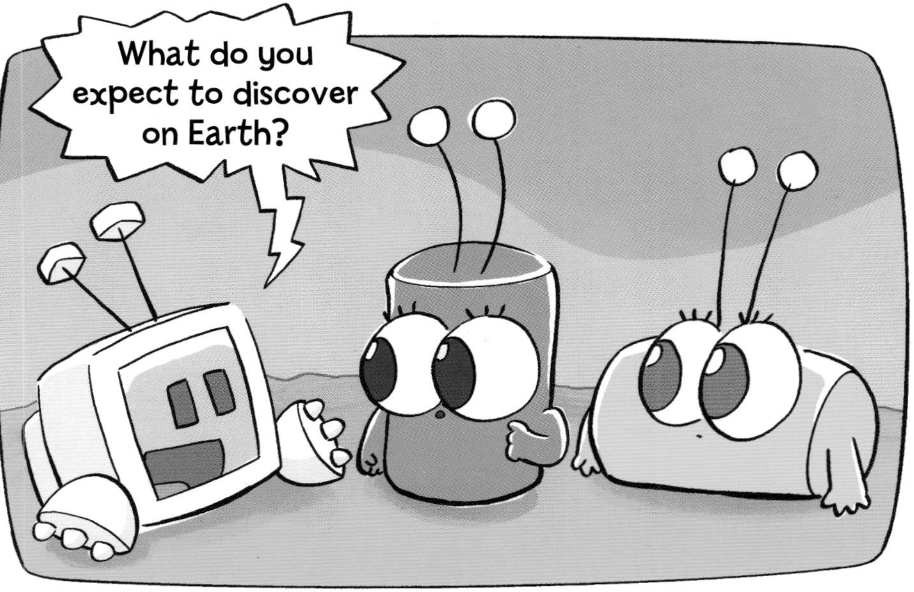
What do you expect to discover on Earth?

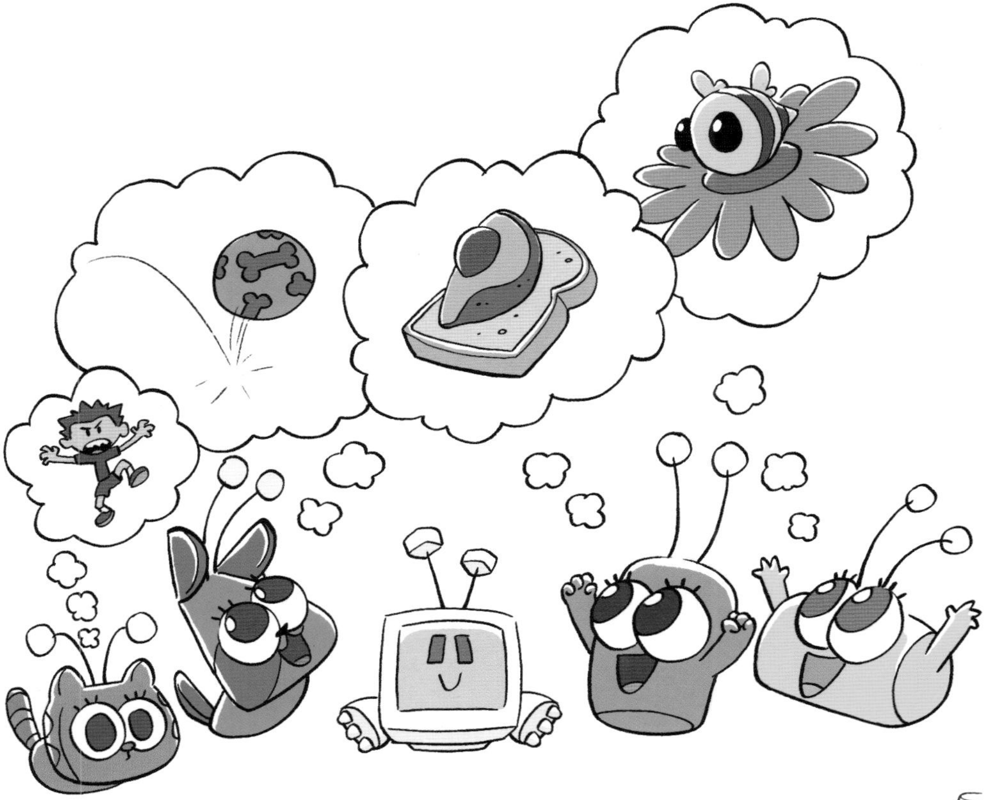

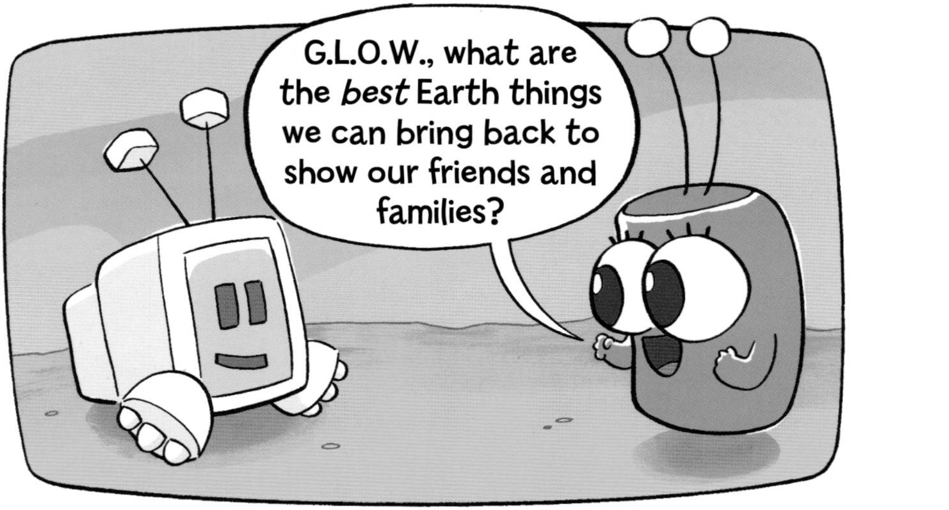
G.L.O.W., what are the *best* Earth things we can bring back to show our friends and families?

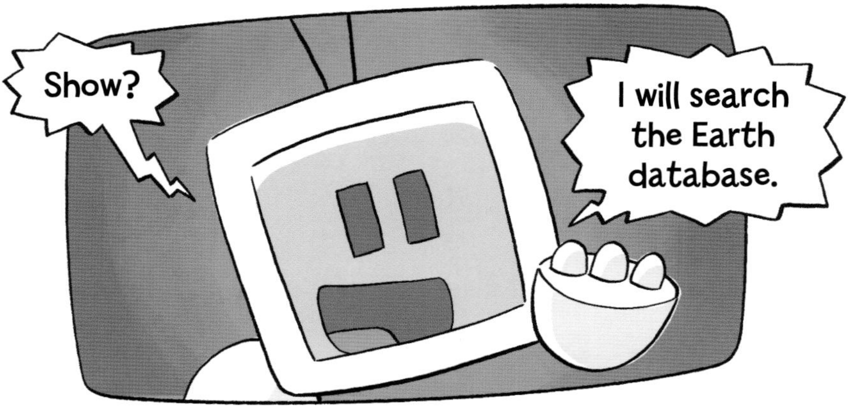
Show?
I will search the Earth database.

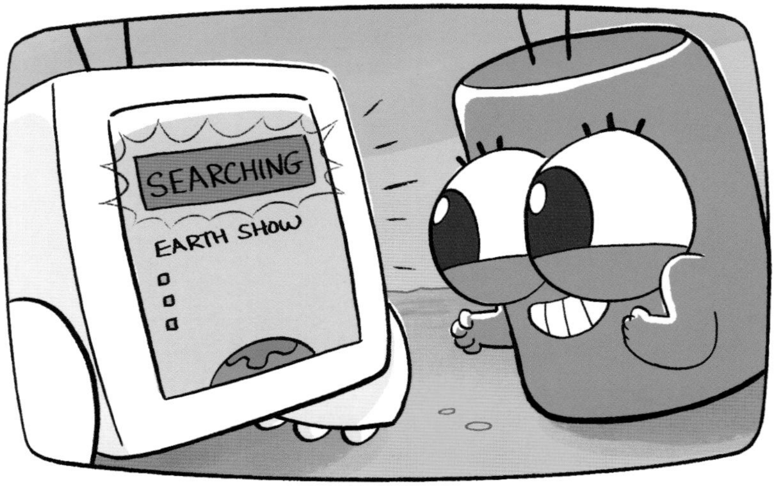
SEARCHING
EARTH SHOW

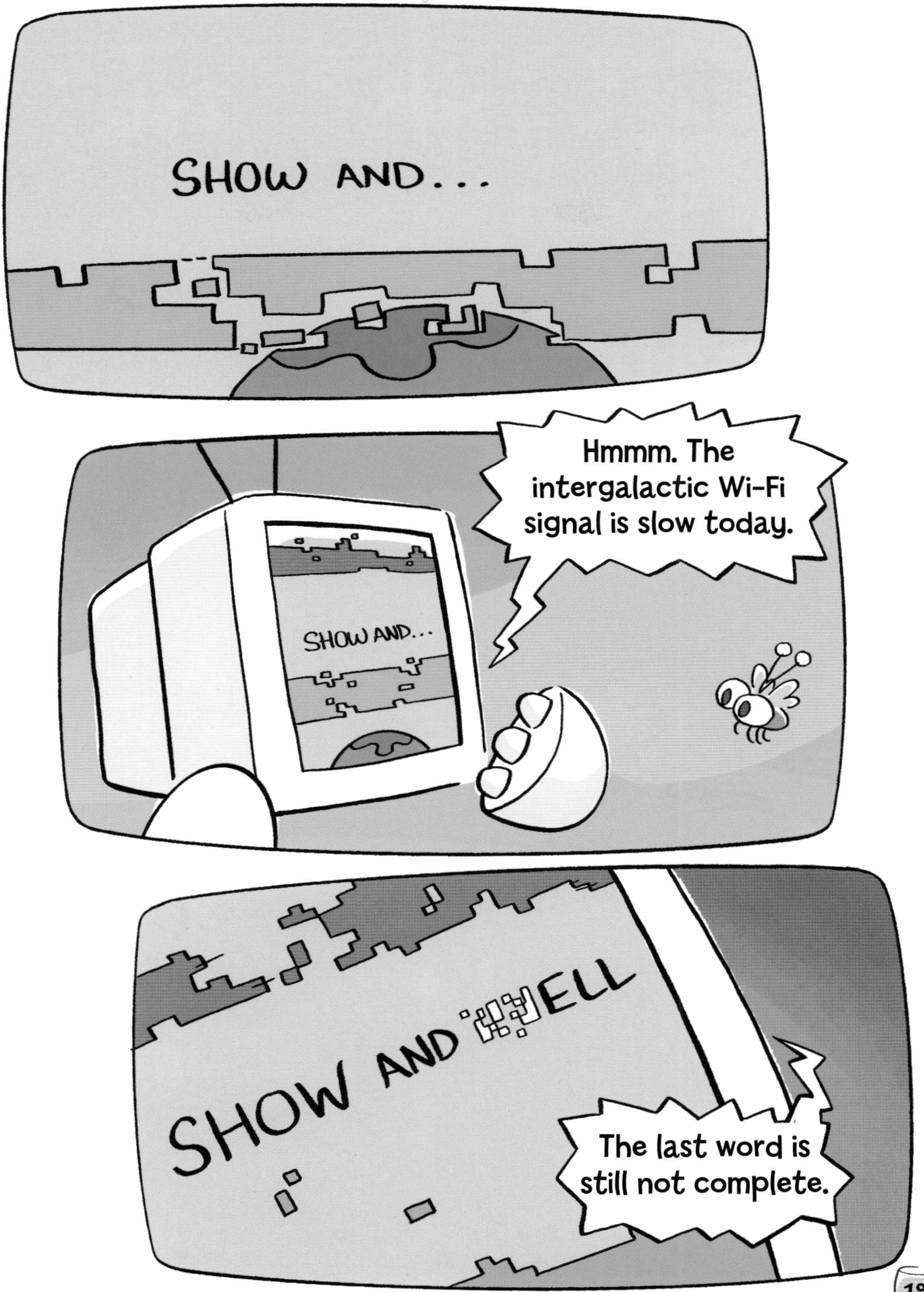
SHOW AND...
Hmmm. The intergalactic Wi-Fi signal is slow today.
SHOW AND...
SHOW AND ELL
The last word is still not complete.

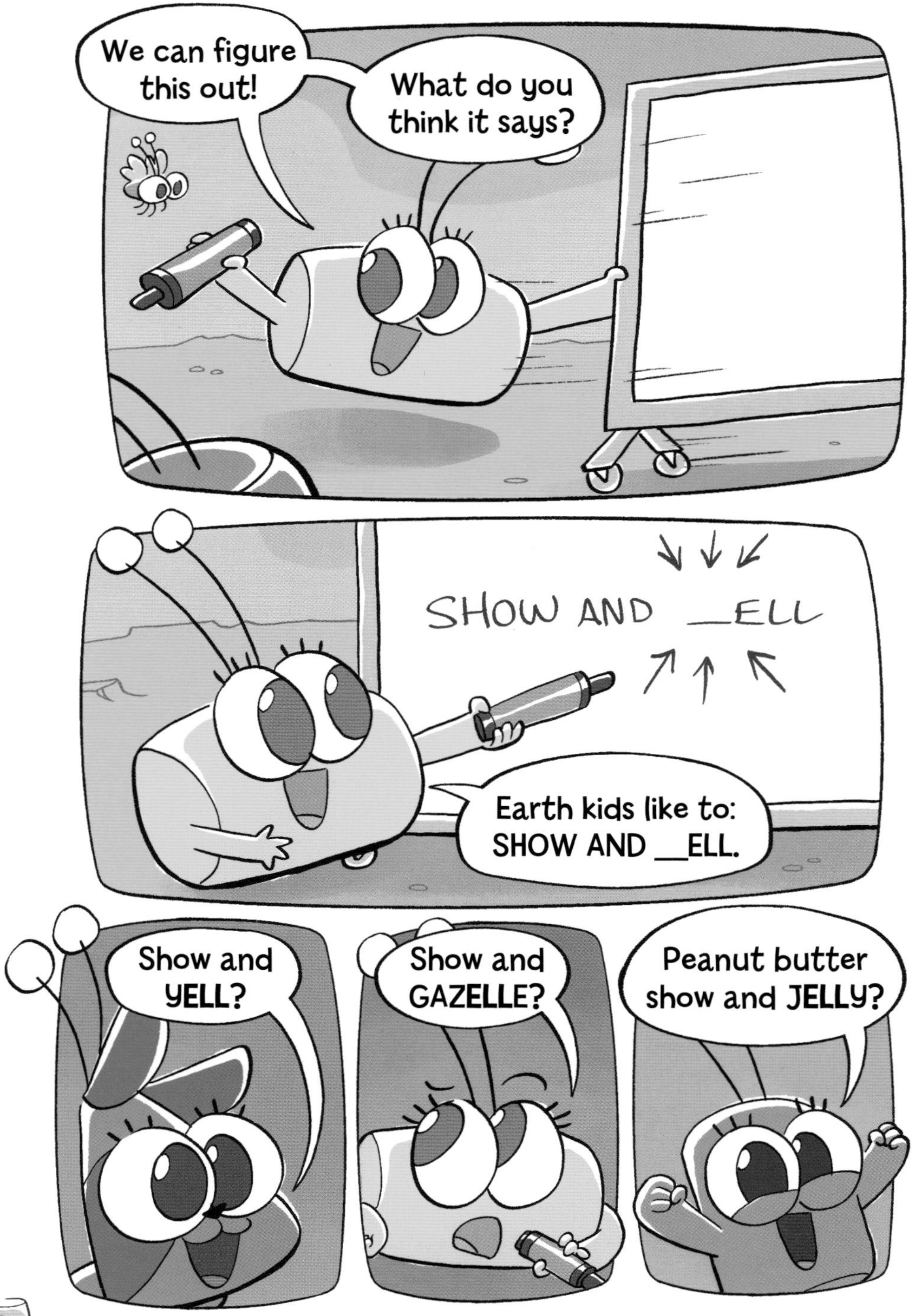

We can figure this out!
What do you think it says?
SHOW AND __ELL
Earth kids like to: SHOW AND __ELL.
Show and YELL?
Show and GAZELLE?
Peanut butter show and JELLY?

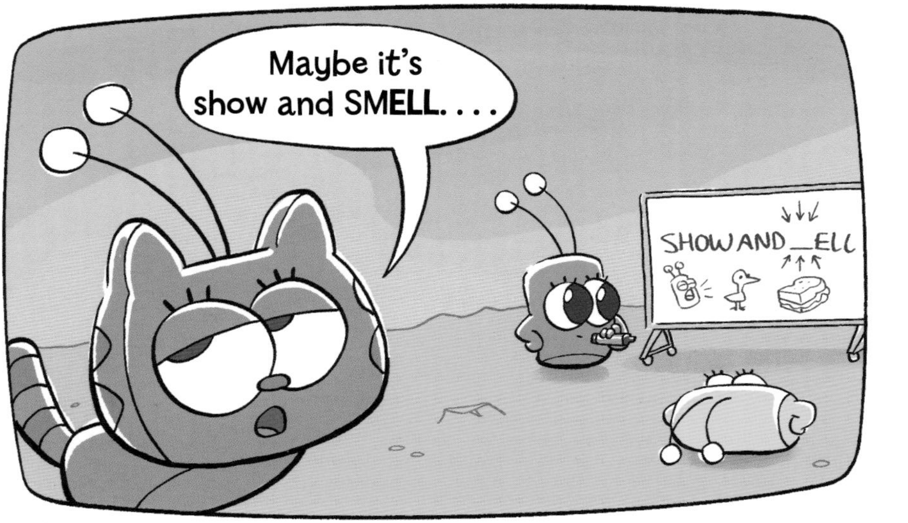
Maybe it's show and SMELL. . . .
SHOW AND __ELL

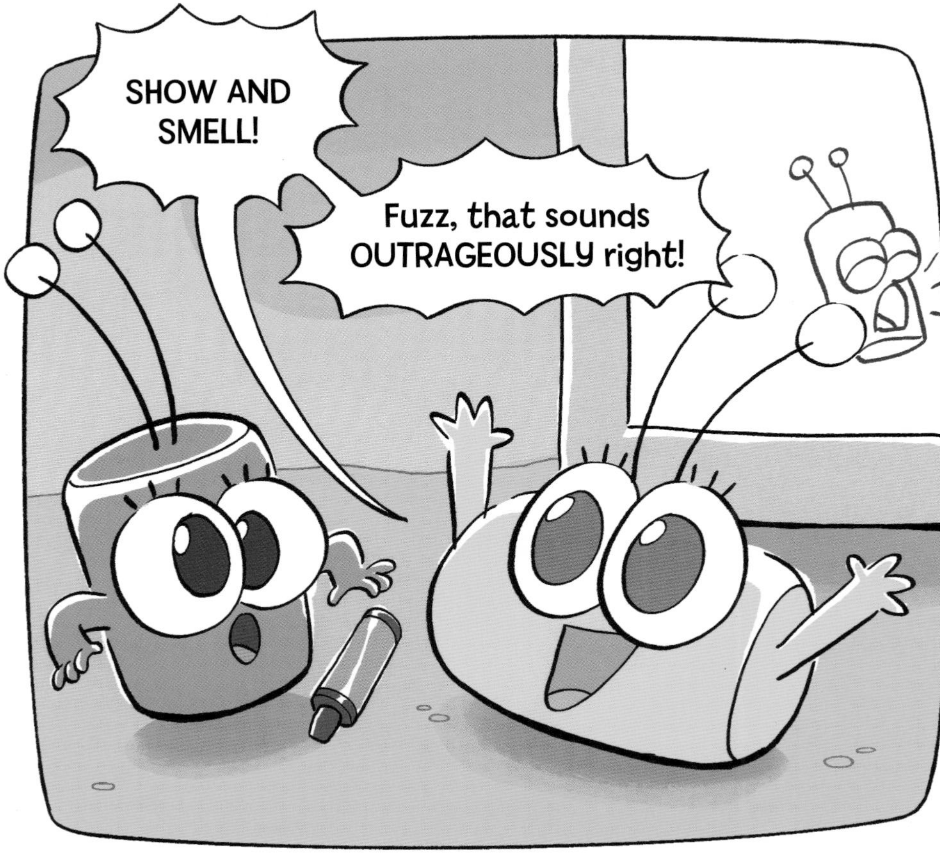
SHOW AND SMELL!
Fuzz, that sounds OUTRAGEOUSLY right!

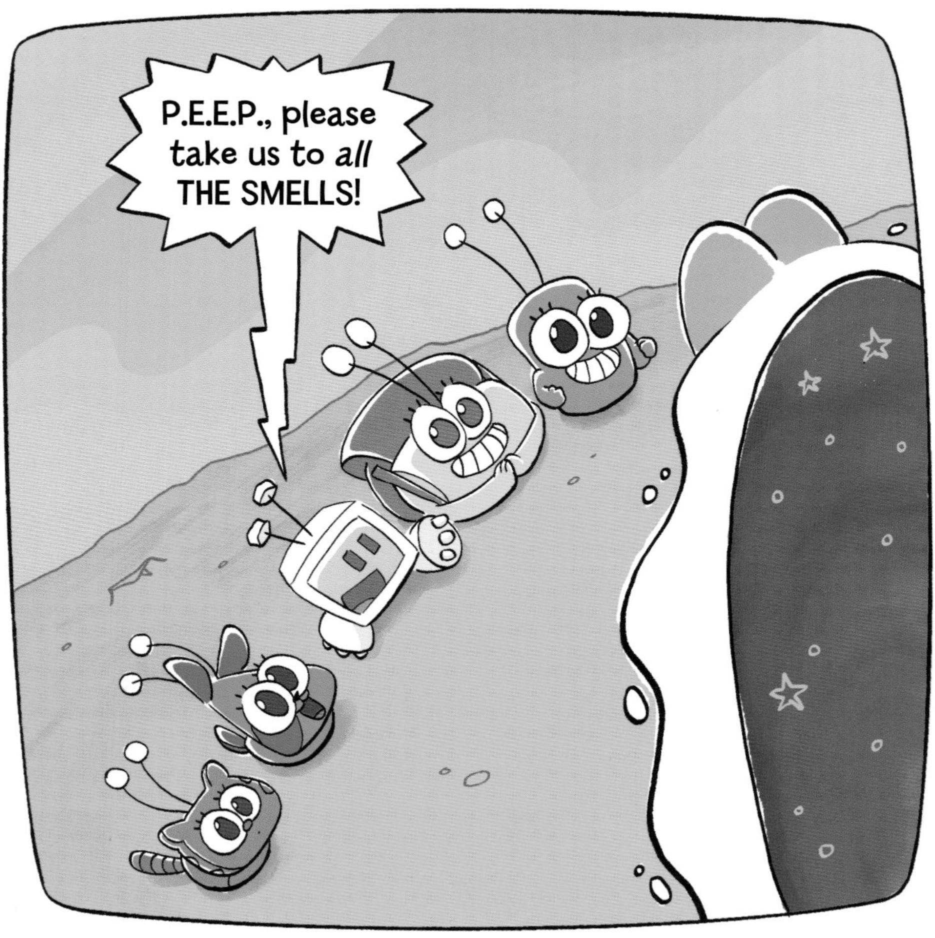
P.E.E.P., please take us to *all* THE SMELLS!

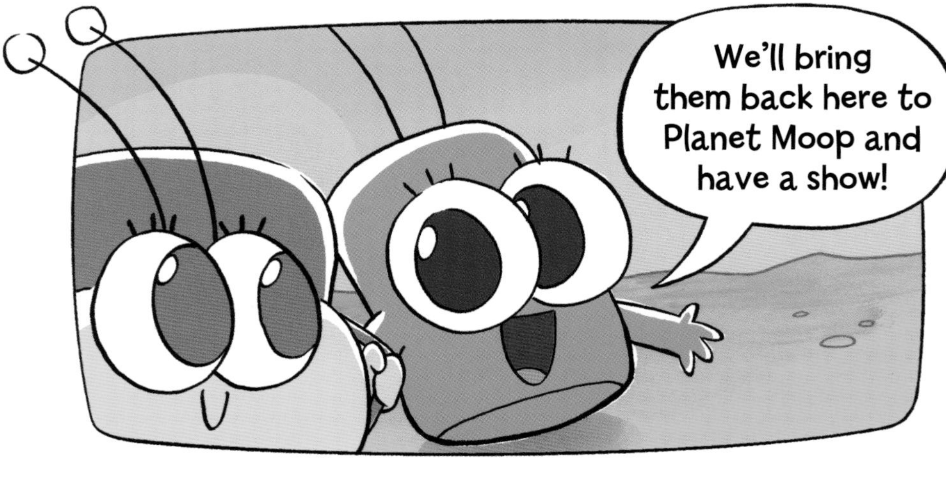
We'll bring them back here to Planet Moop and have a show!

Chapter 4

First Mission!

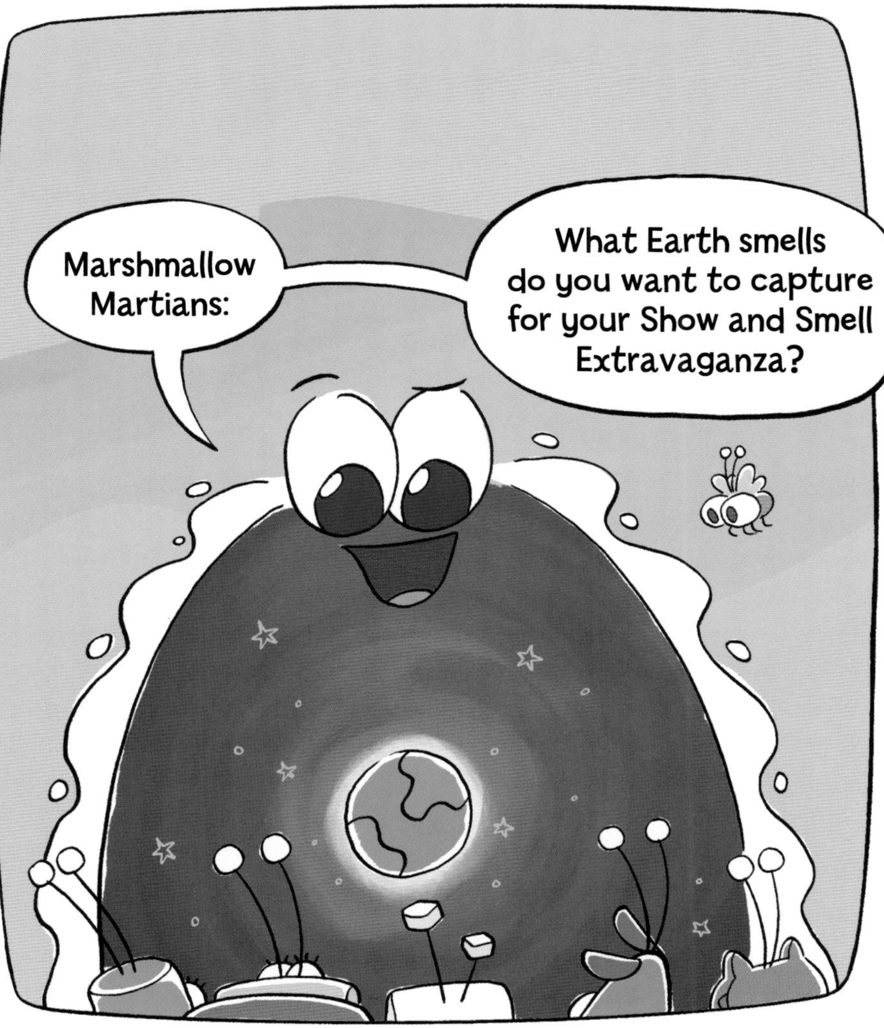
Marshmallow Martians:
What Earth smells do you want to capture for your Show and Smell Extravaganza?

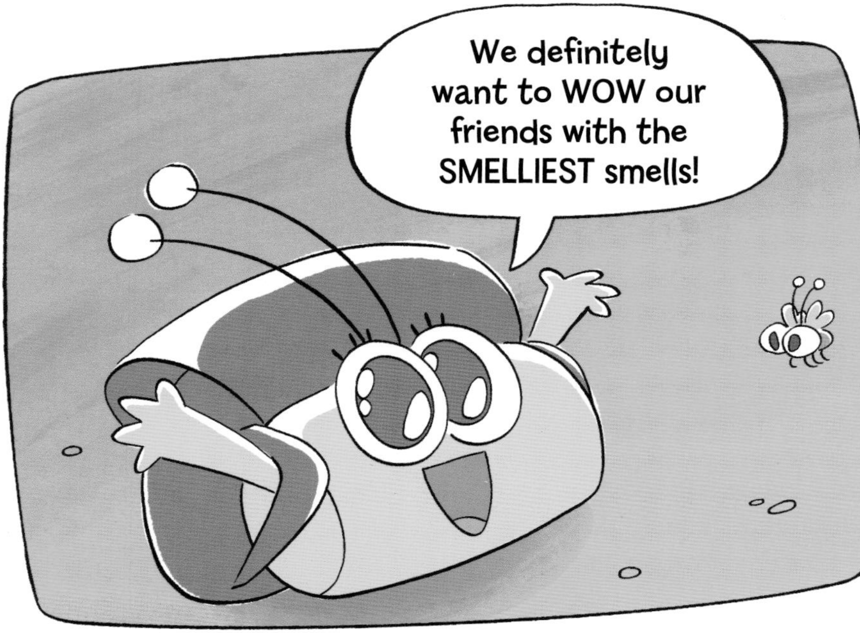
We definitely want to WOW our friends with the SMELLIEST smells!

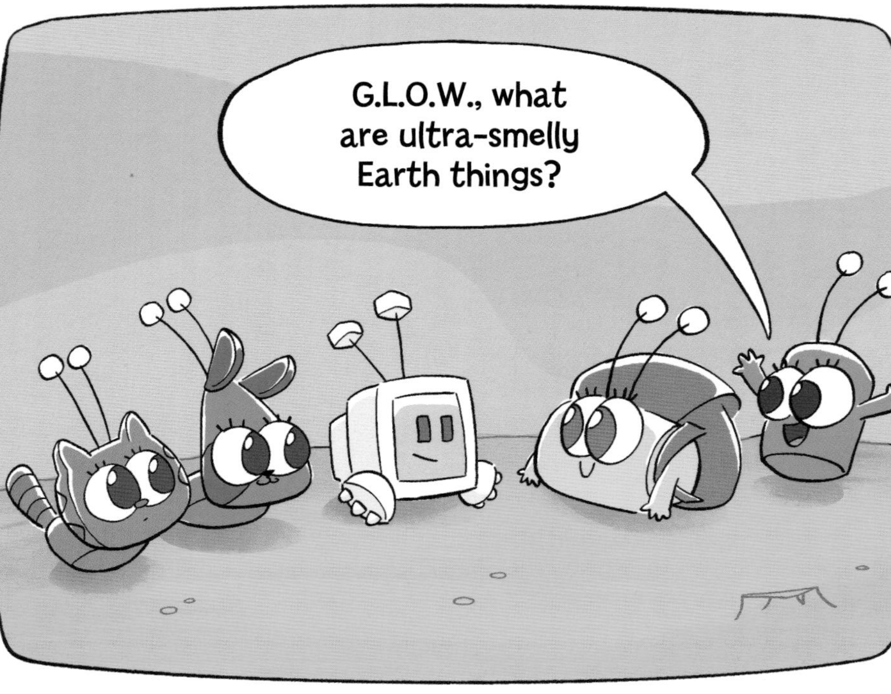
G.L.O.W., what are ultra-smelly Earth things?

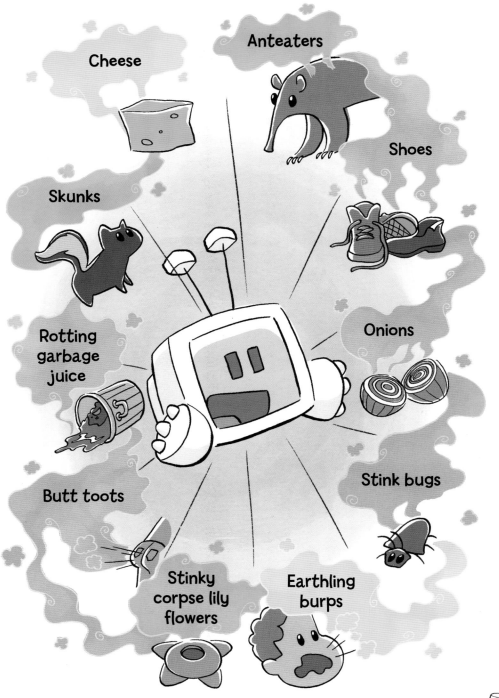

Cheese

Anteaters

Shoes

Skunks

Rotting garbage juice

Onions

Butt toots

Stink bugs

Stinky corpse lily flowers

Earthling burps

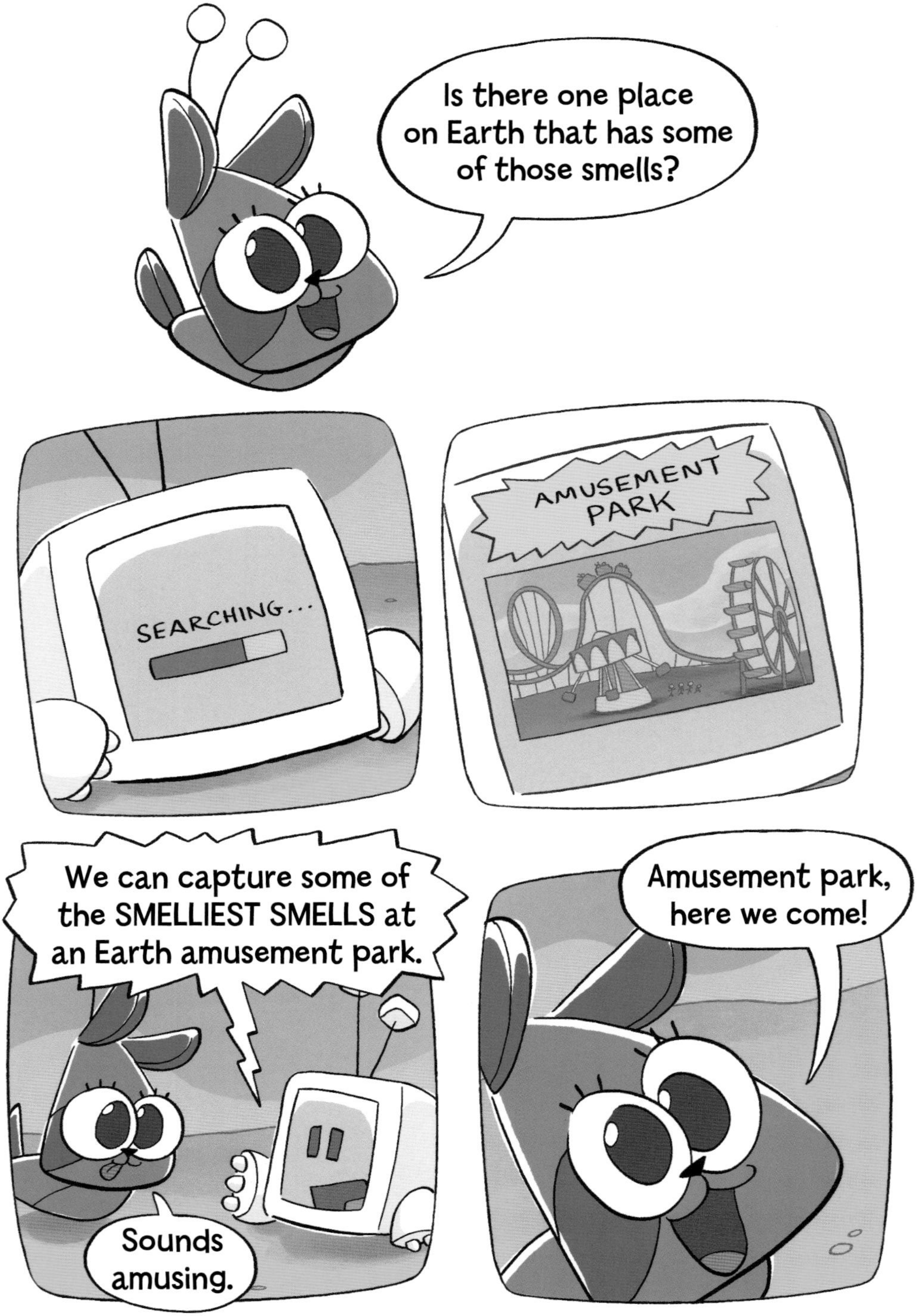
Is there one place on Earth that has some of those smells?
SEARCHING...
AMUSEMENT PARK
We can capture some of the SMELLIEST SMELLS at an Earth amusement park.
Sounds amusing.
Amusement park, here we come!

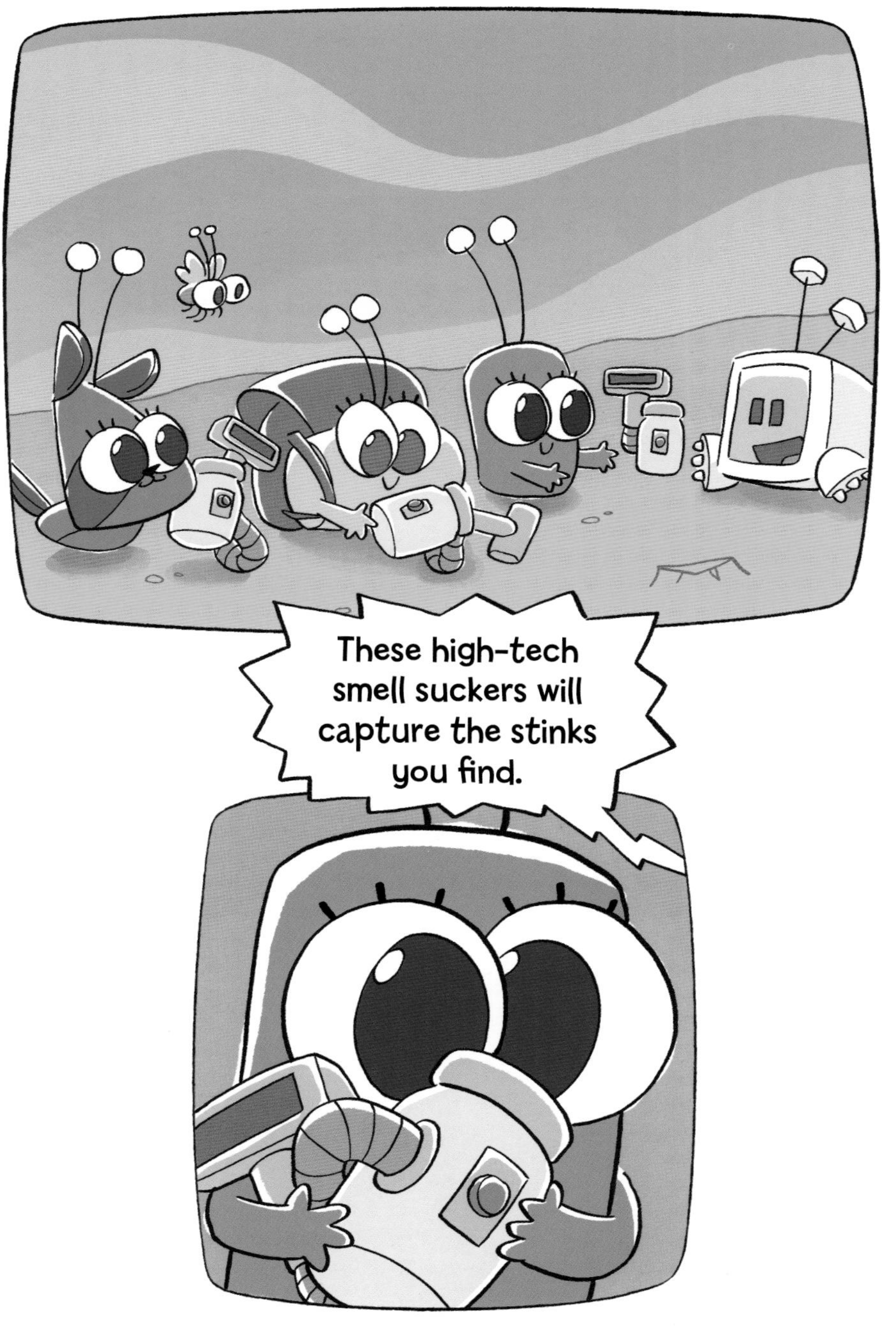
These high-tech smell suckers will capture the stinks you find.

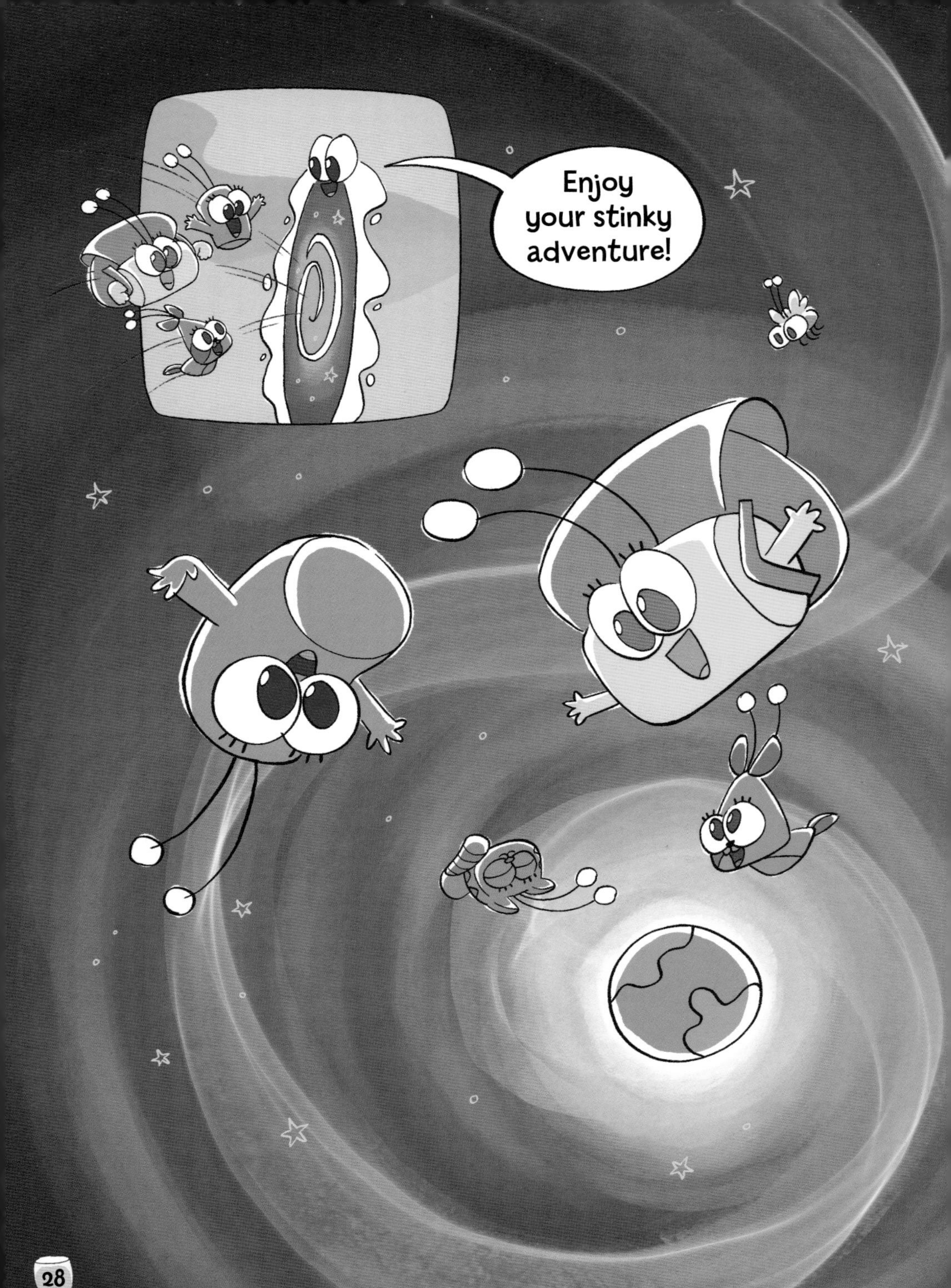
Enjoy your stinky adventure!

Chapter 5
Capture the Shoe Stench!

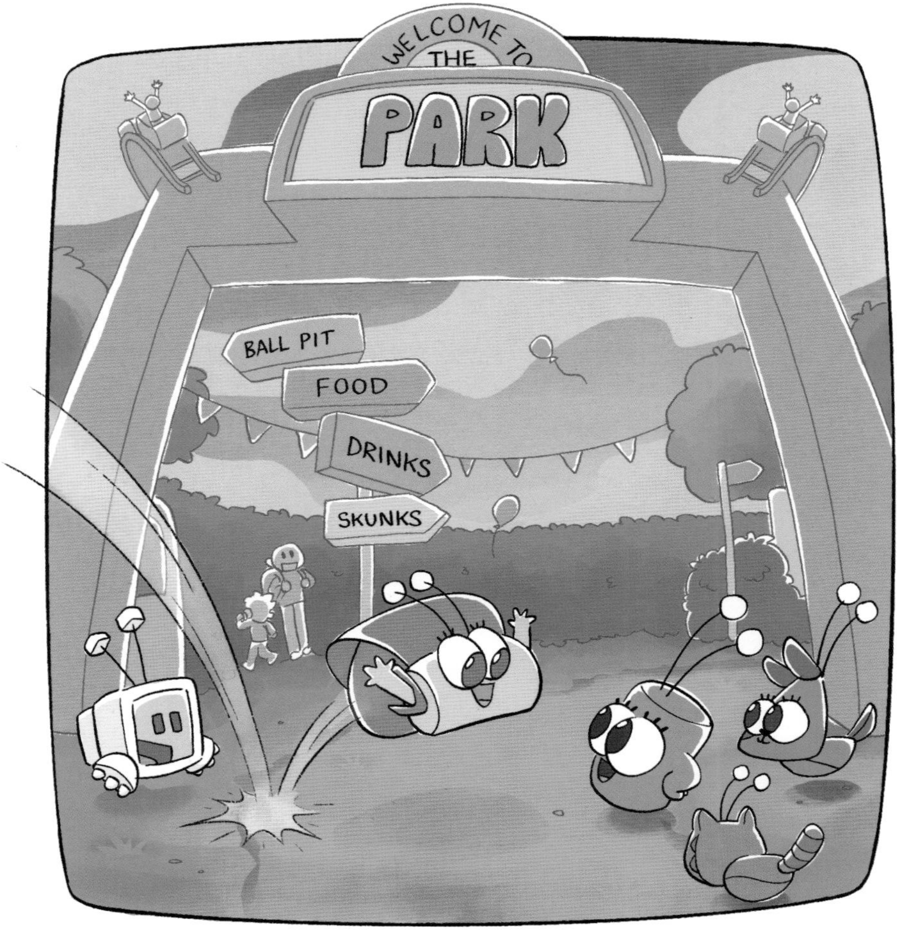
WELCOME TO
THE
PARK
BALL PIT
FOOD
DRINKS
SKUNKS

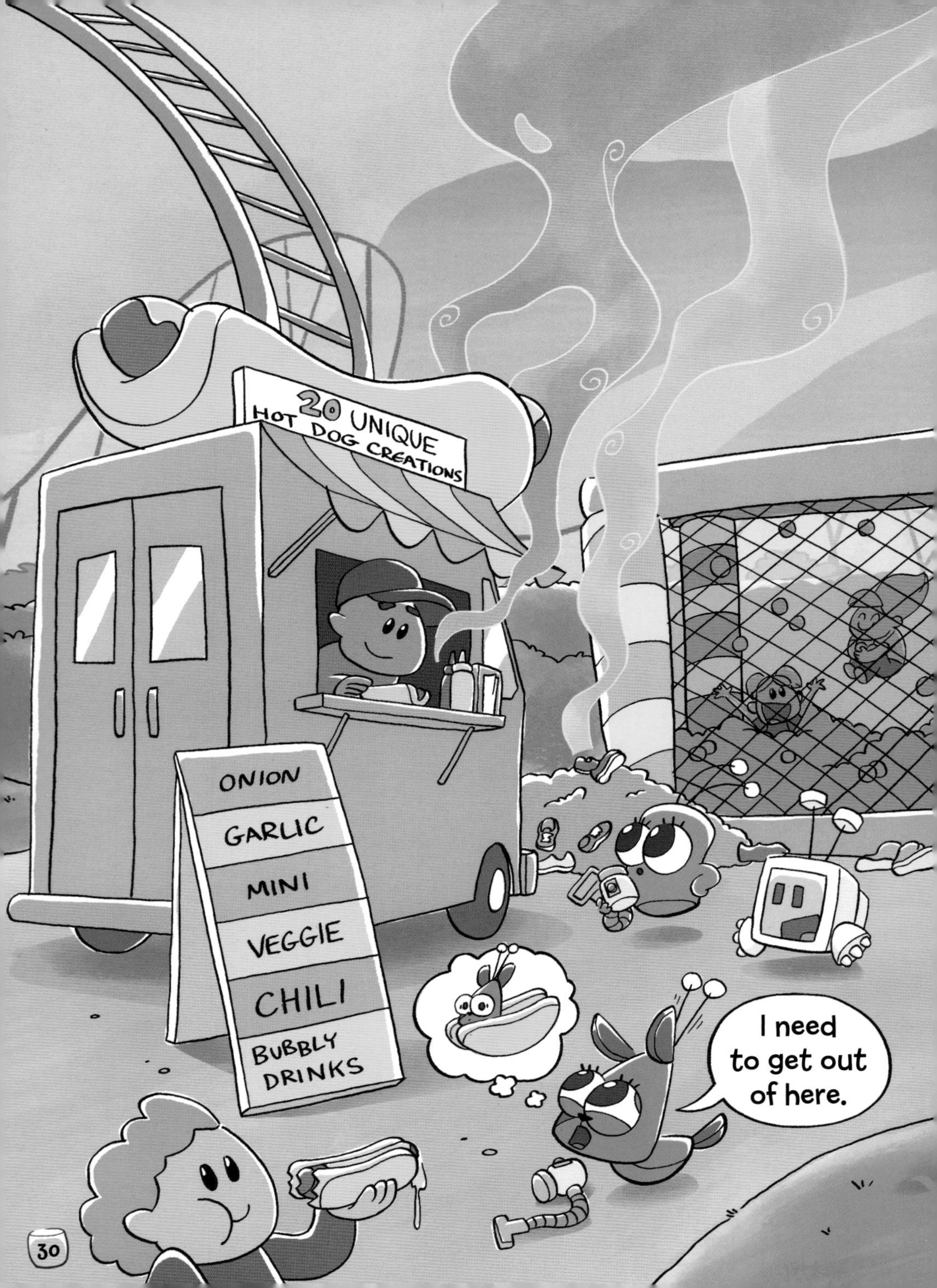
20 UNIQUE HOT DOG CREATIONS
ONION
GARLIC
MINI
VEGGIE
CHILI
BUBBLY DRINKS
I need to get out of here.

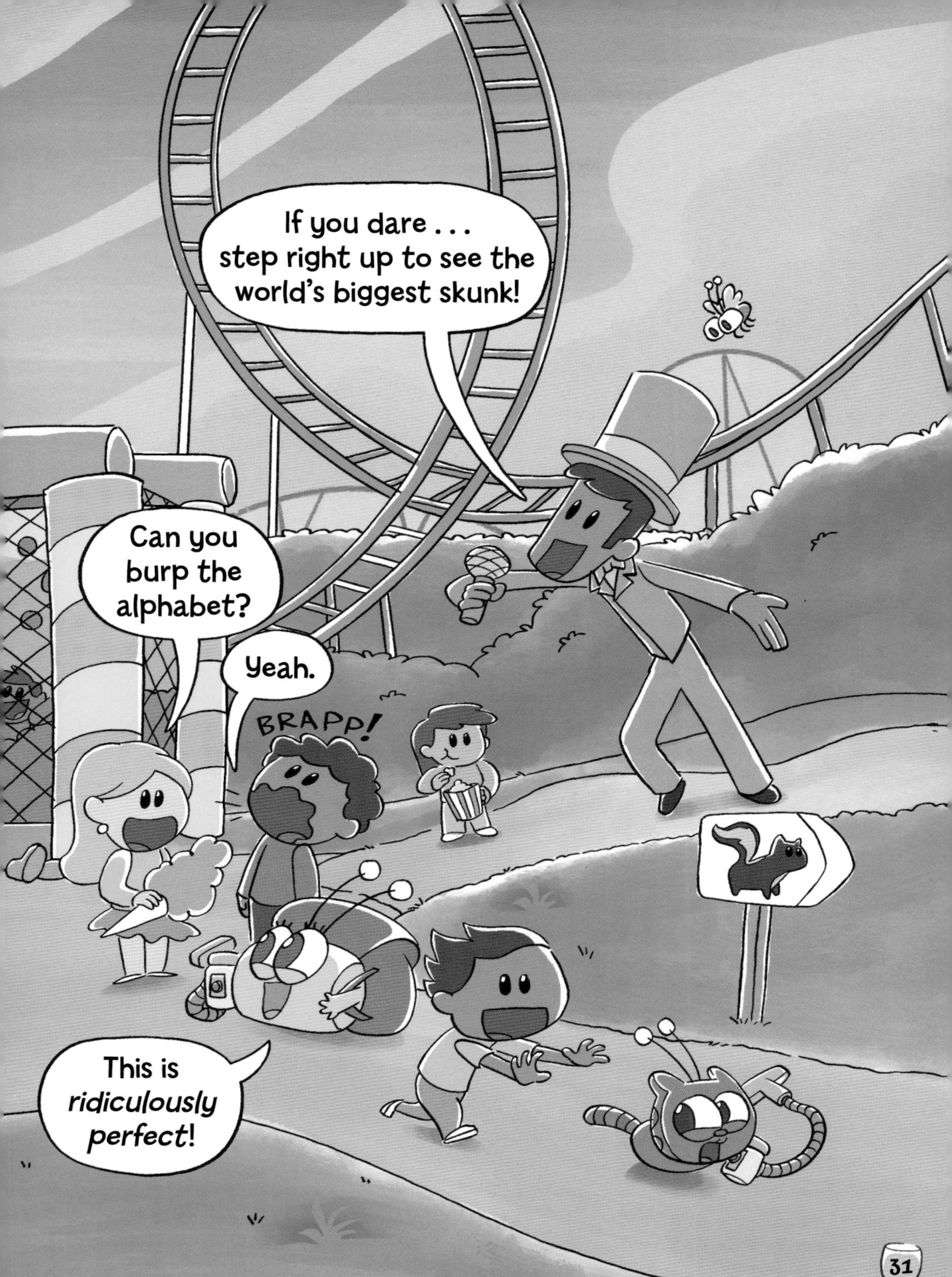
If you dare . . . step right up to see the world's biggest skunk!
Can you burp the alphabet?
Yeah.
BRAPP!
This is *ridiculously* *perfect*!

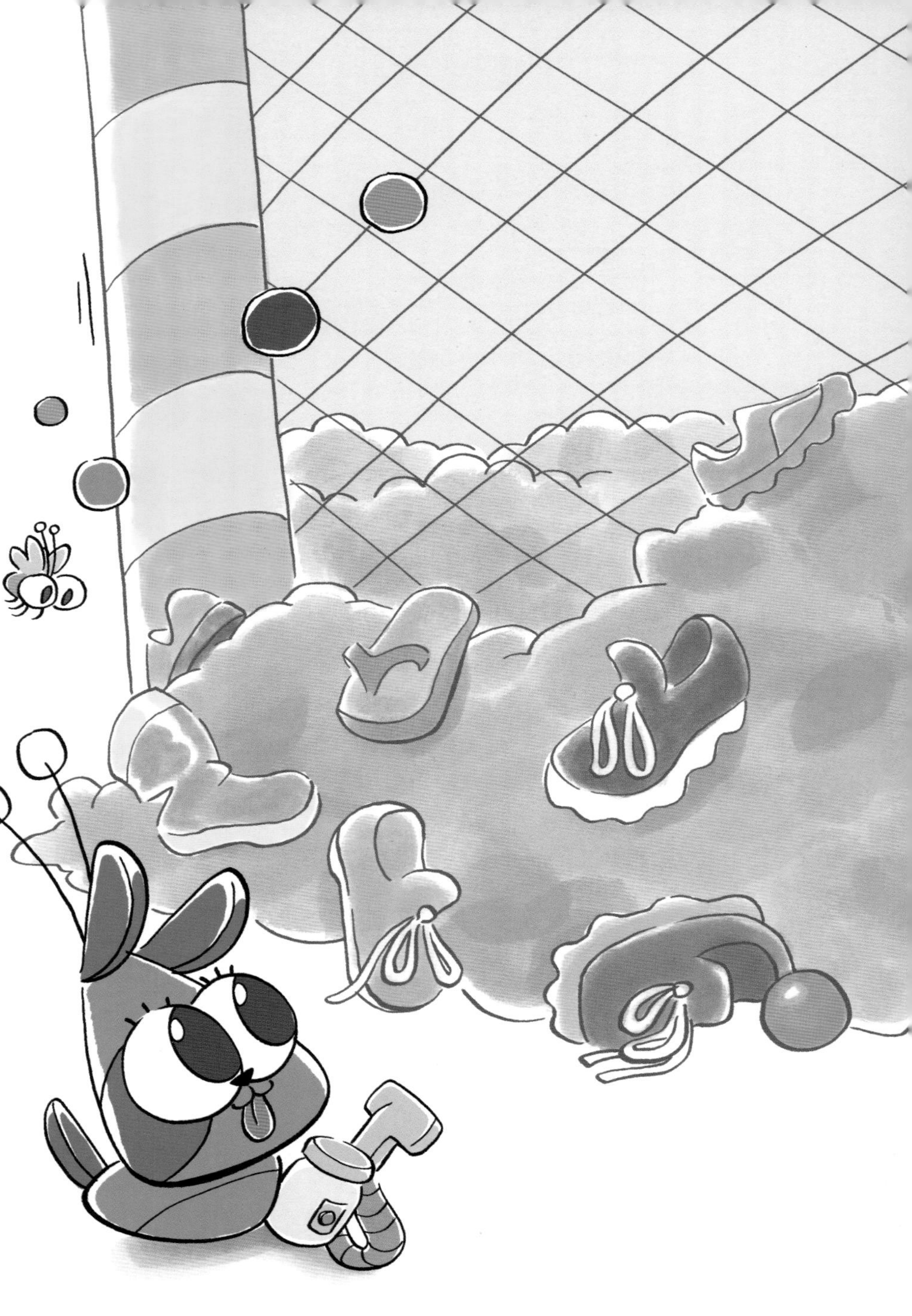

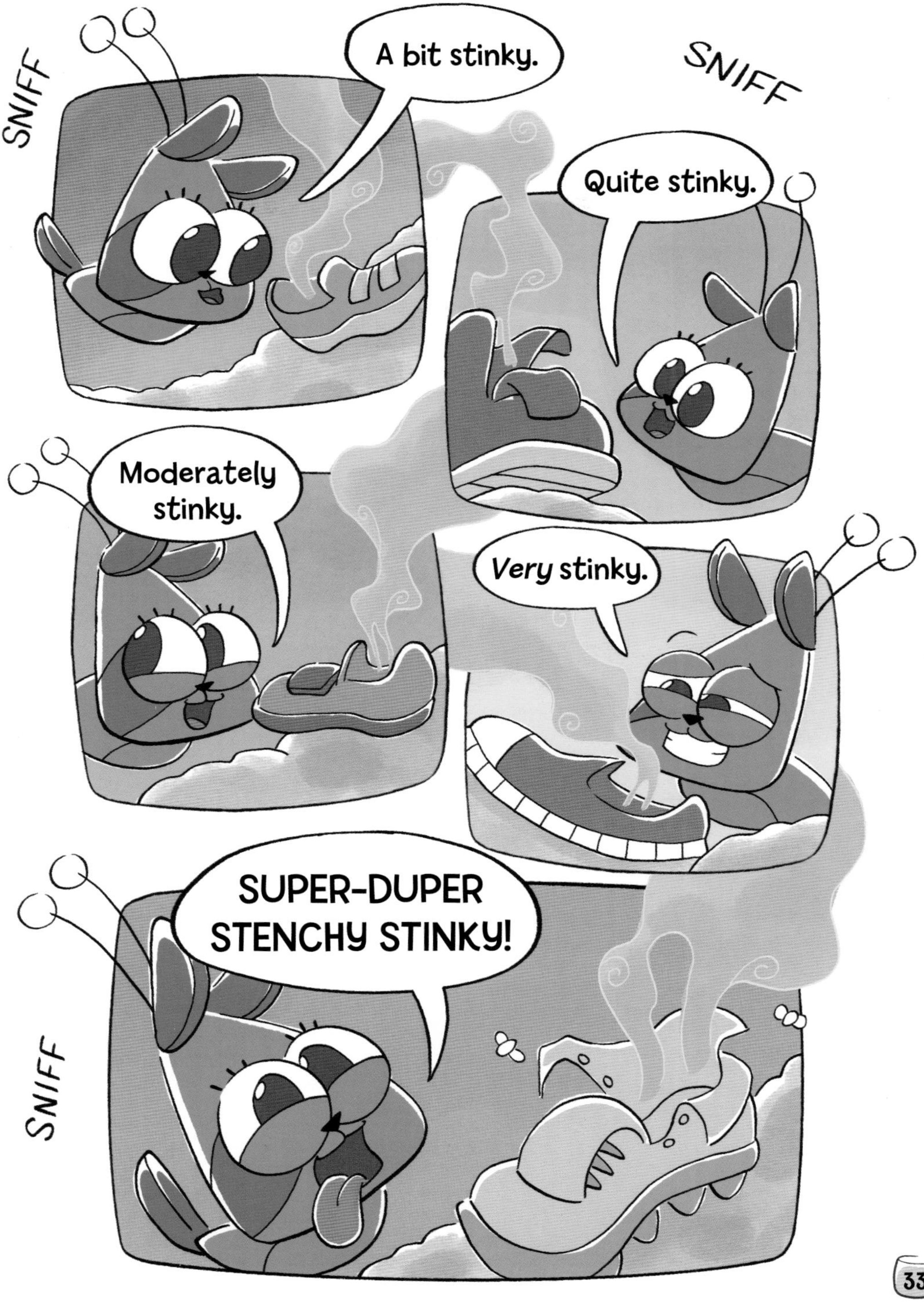
SNIFF
A bit stinky.
SNIFF
Quite stinky.
Moderately stinky.
Very stinky.
SUPER-DUPER STENCHY STINKY!
SNIFF

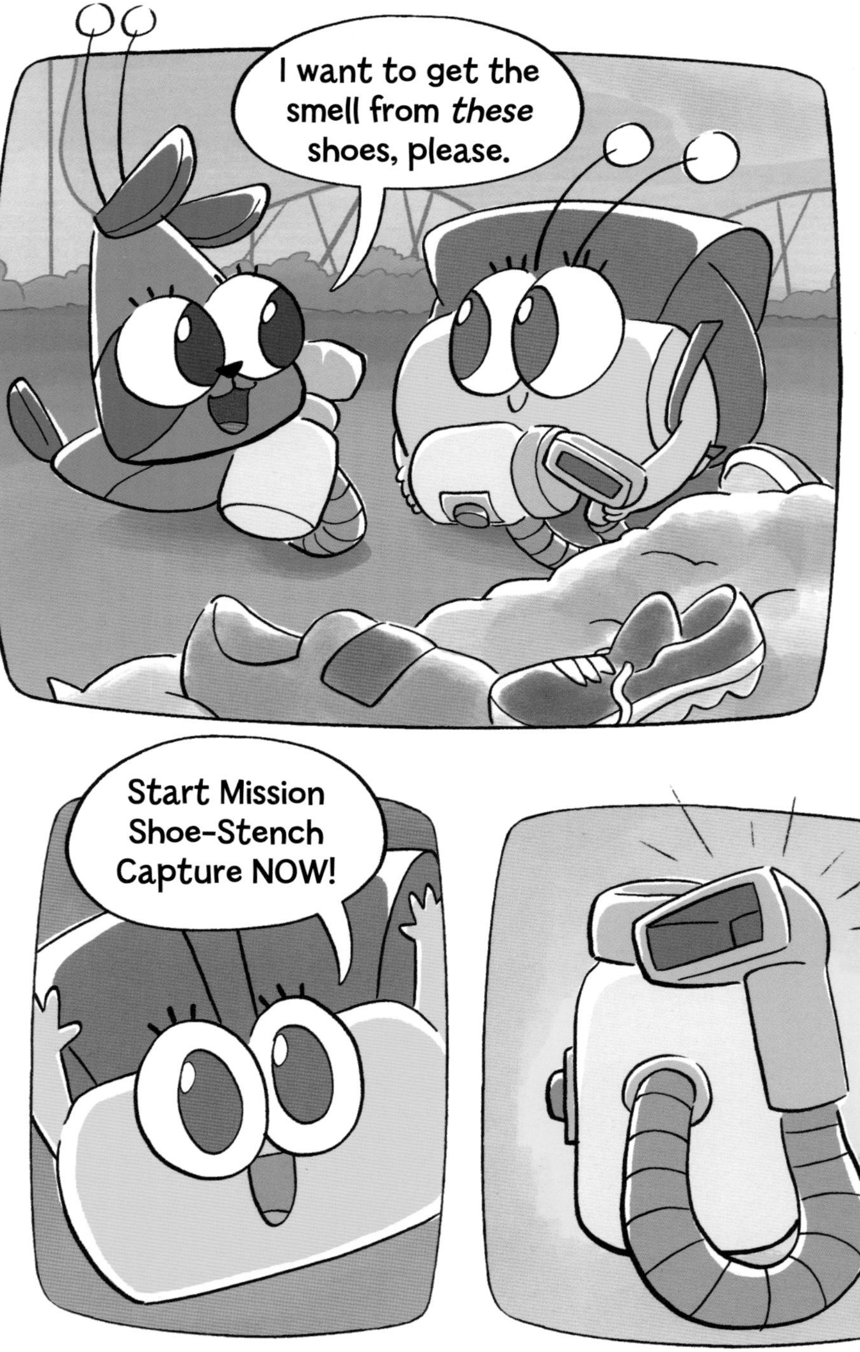
I want to get the smell from *these* shoes, please.
Start Mission Shoe-Stench Capture NOW!

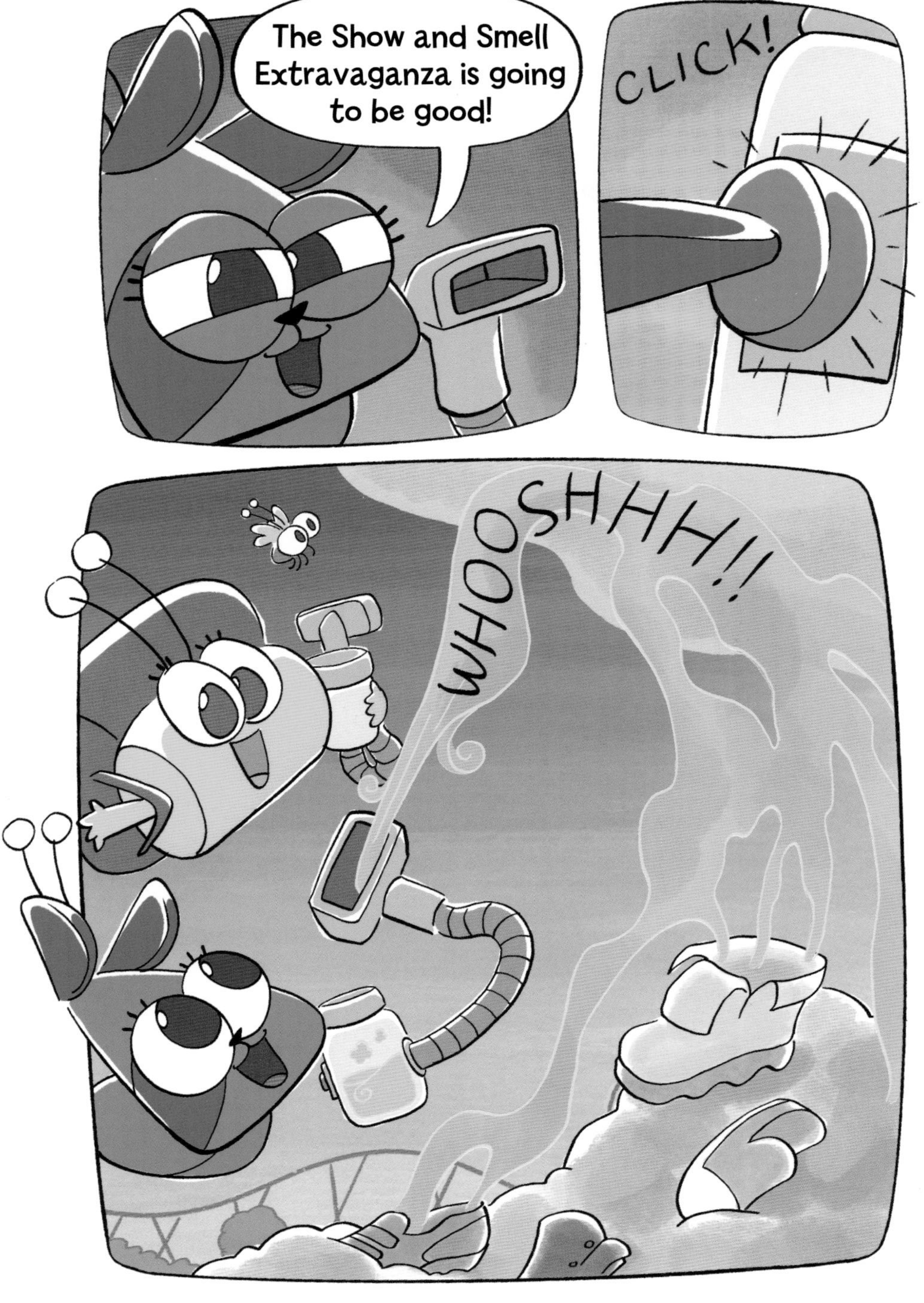
The Show and Smell Extravaganza is going to be good!
CLICK!
WHOOSHHH!!

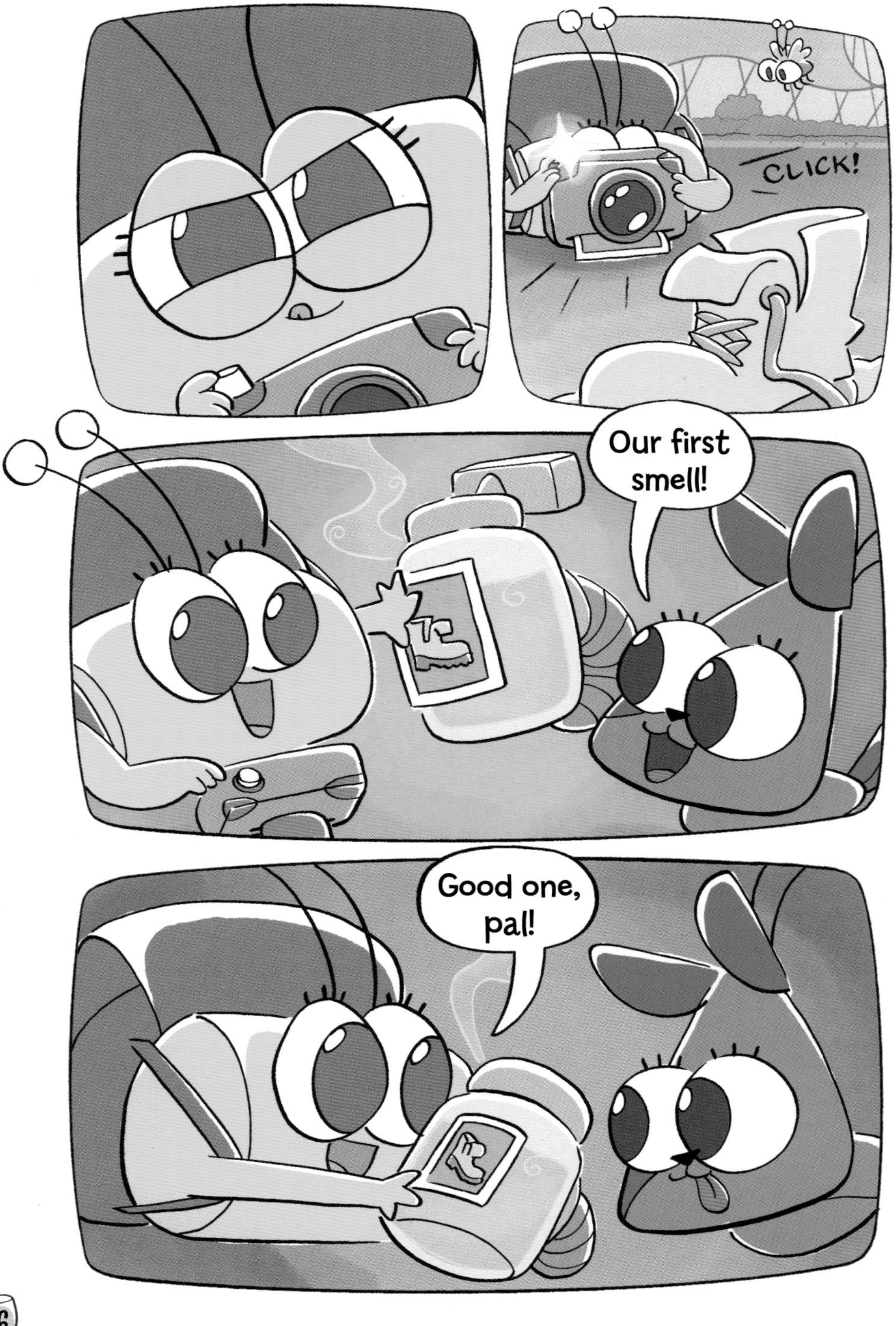
CLICK!
Our first smell!
Good one, pal!

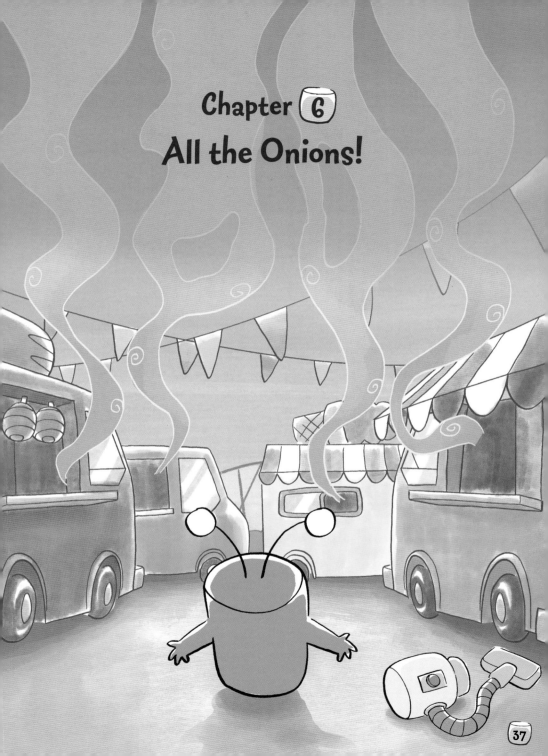

Chapter 6
All the Onions!

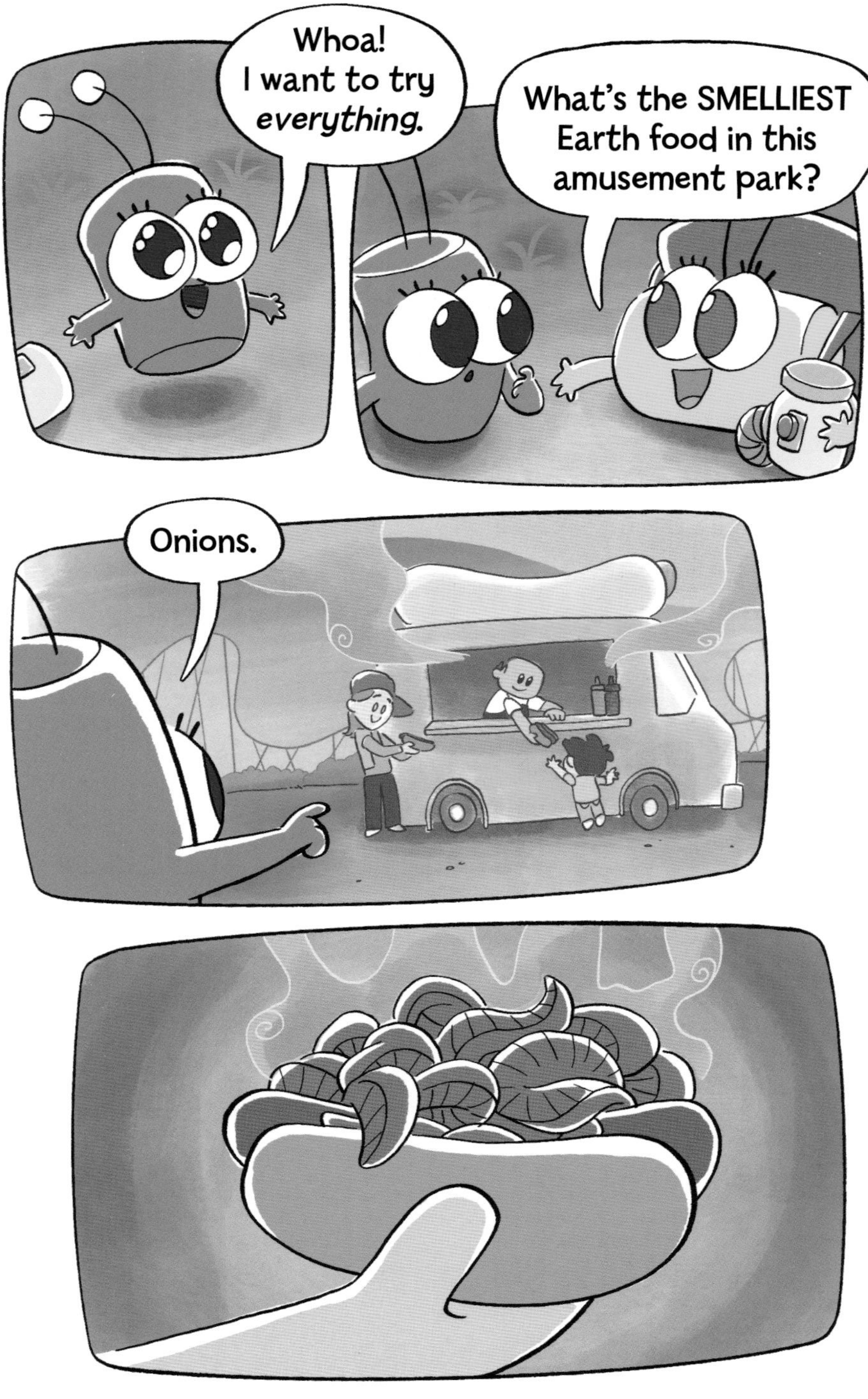
Whoa!
I want to try *everything.*
What's the SMELLIEST Earth food in this amusement park?
Onions.

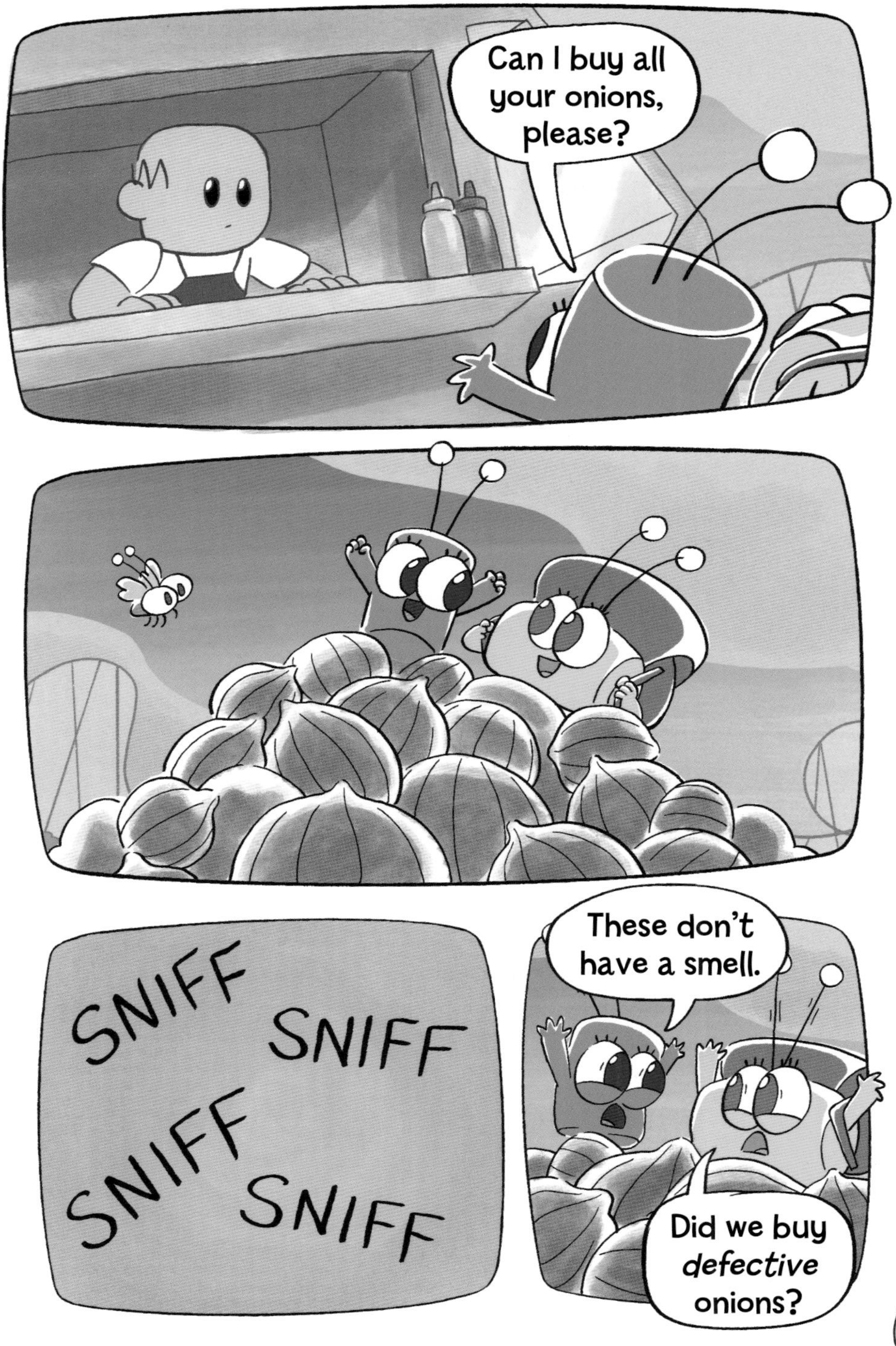
Can I buy all your onions, please?
SNIFF
SNIFF
SNIFF
SNIFF
These don't have a smell.
Did we buy *defective* onions?

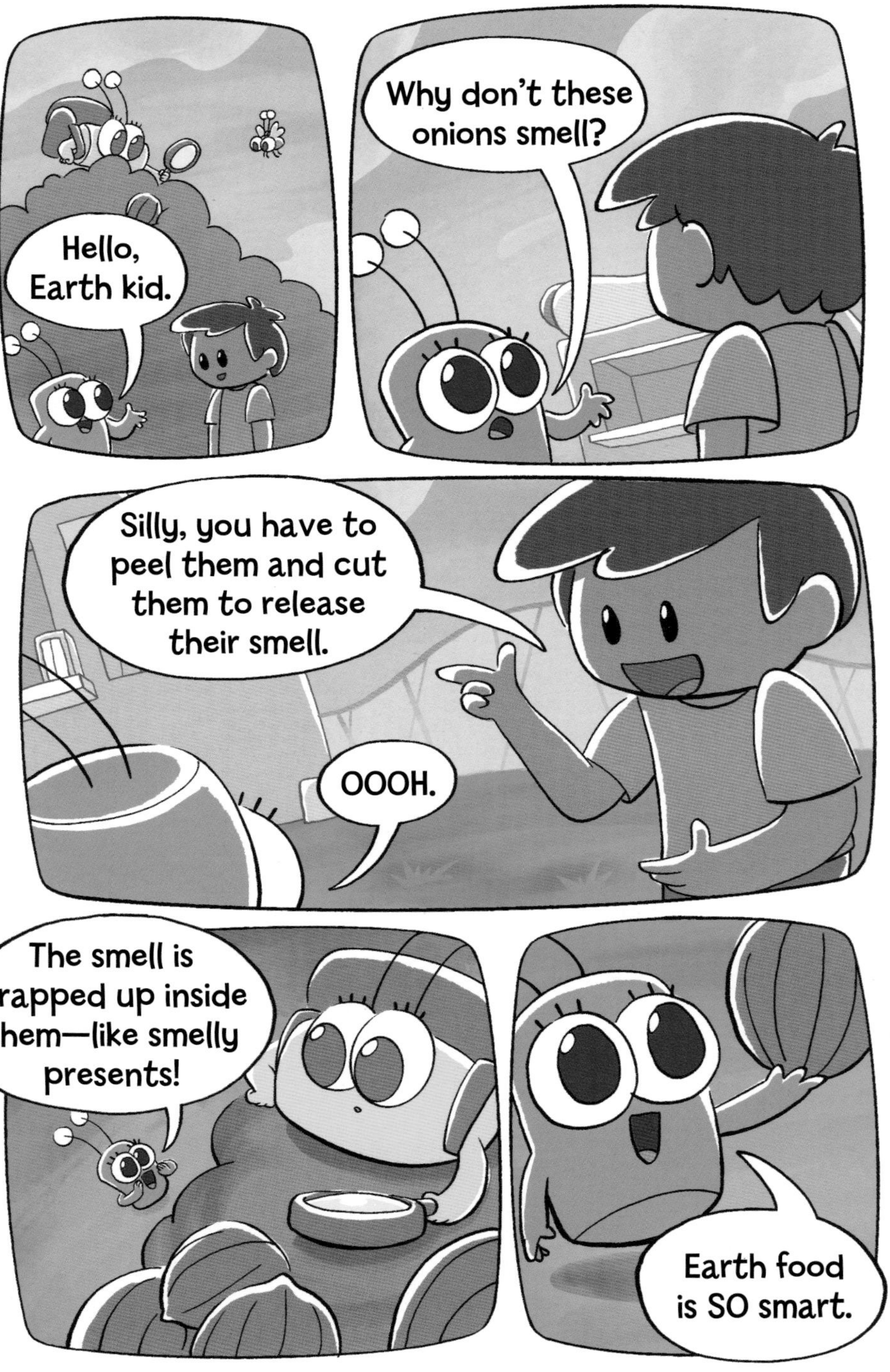

Hello, Earth kid.
Why don't these onions smell?
Silly, you have to peel them and cut them to release their smell.
OOOH.
The smell is wrapped up inside them—like smelly presents!
Earth food is SO smart.

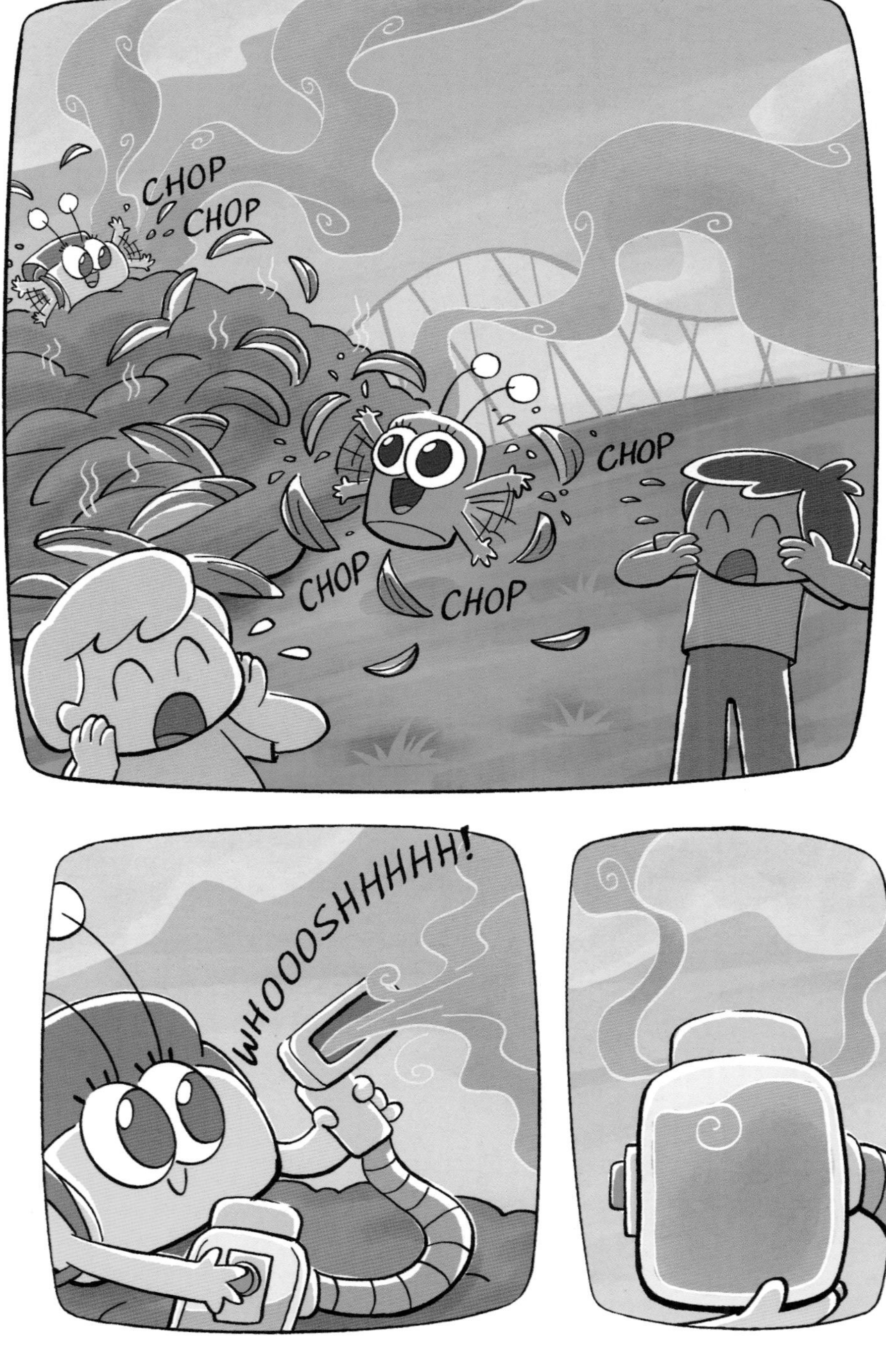
CHOP
CHOP
CHOP
CHOP
CHOP
WHOOOSHHHHH!

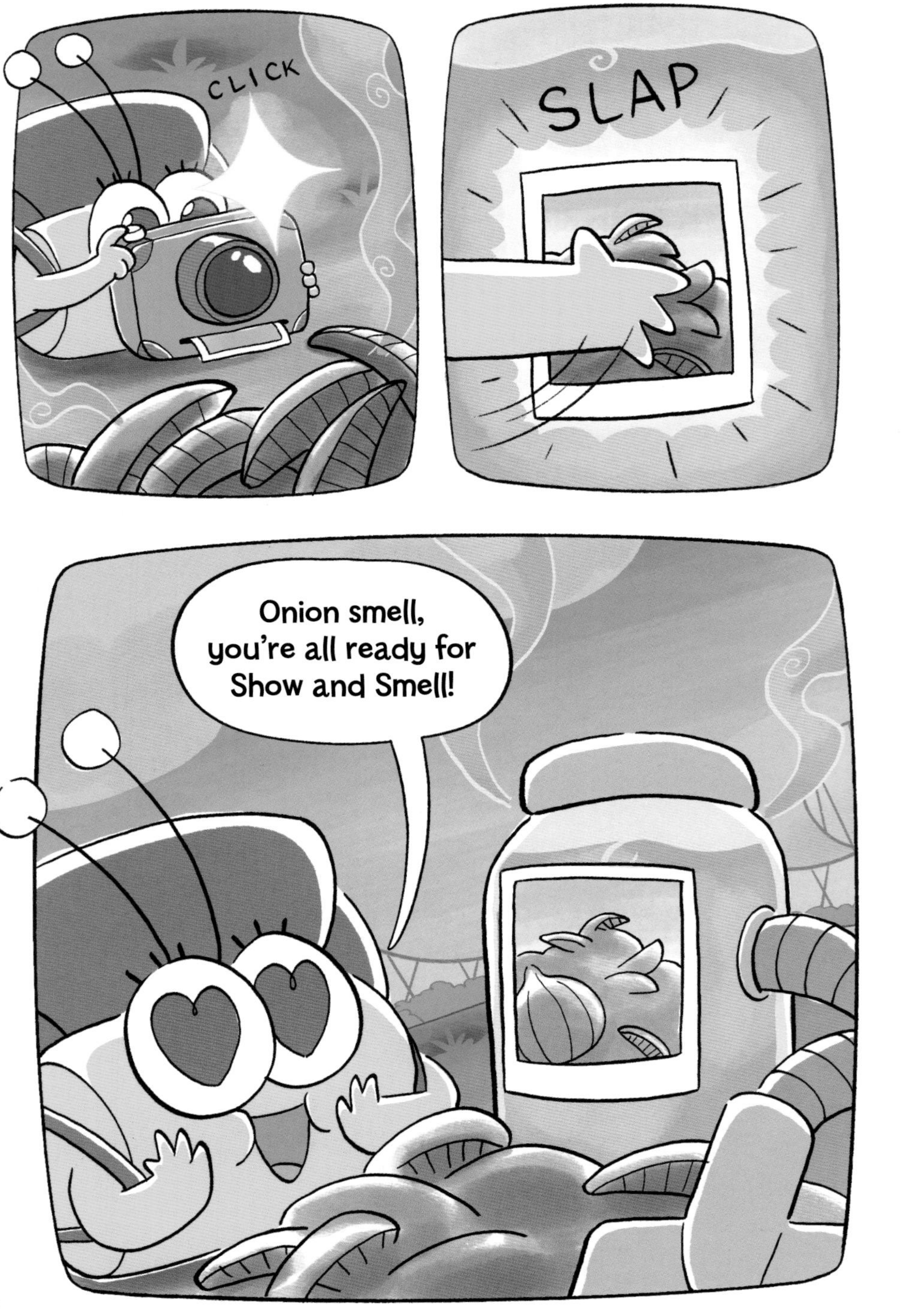
CLICK
SLAP
Onion smell, you're all ready for Show and Smell!

Chapter 7
Capture That Burp!

Earthling burps: I'm coming after you.

Psst! What is a burp?

If Earthlings swallow too much air, it needs to escape.

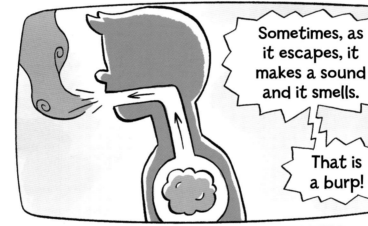

Sometimes, as it escapes, it makes a sound and it smells.

That is a burp!

So Earthling bodies are air jails?

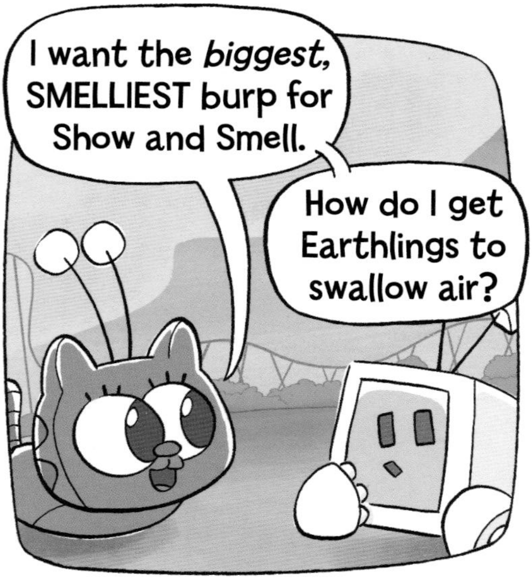
I want the *biggest,* SMELLIEST burp for Show and Smell.
How do I get Earthlings to swallow air?

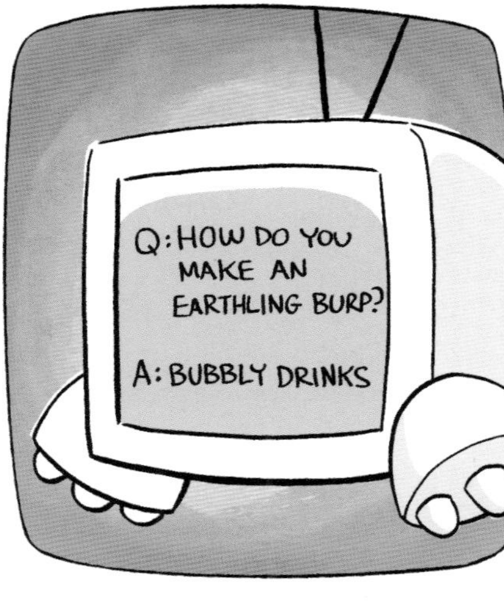
Q: HOW DO YOU MAKE AN EARTHLING BURP?
A: BUBBLY DRINKS

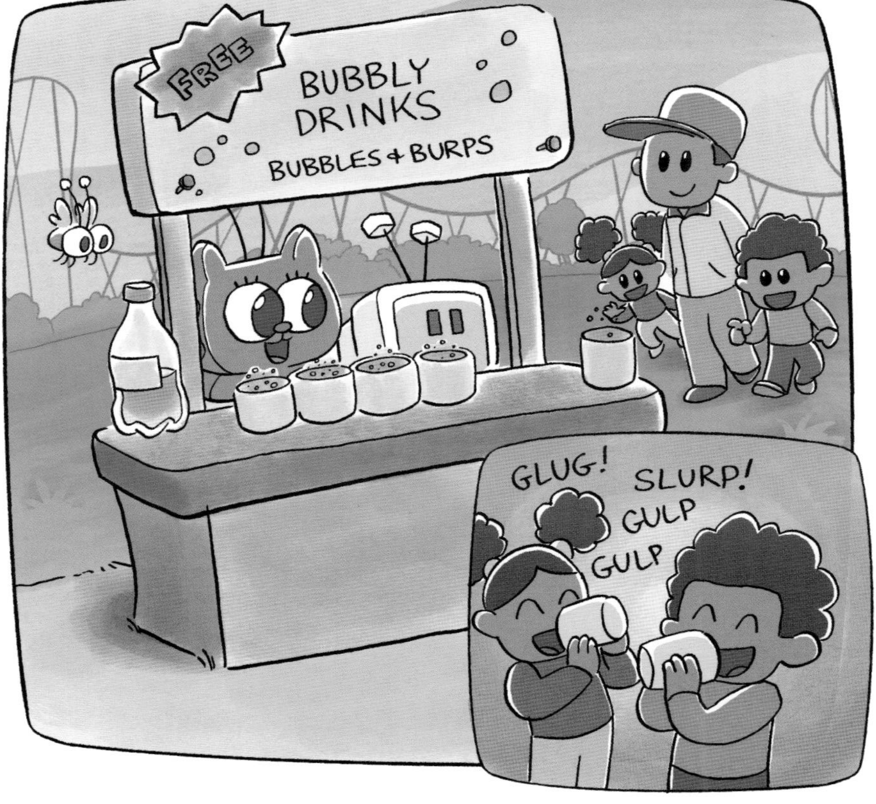
FREE
BUBBLY DRINKS
BUBBLES & BURPS
GLUG!
SLURP!
GULP
GULP

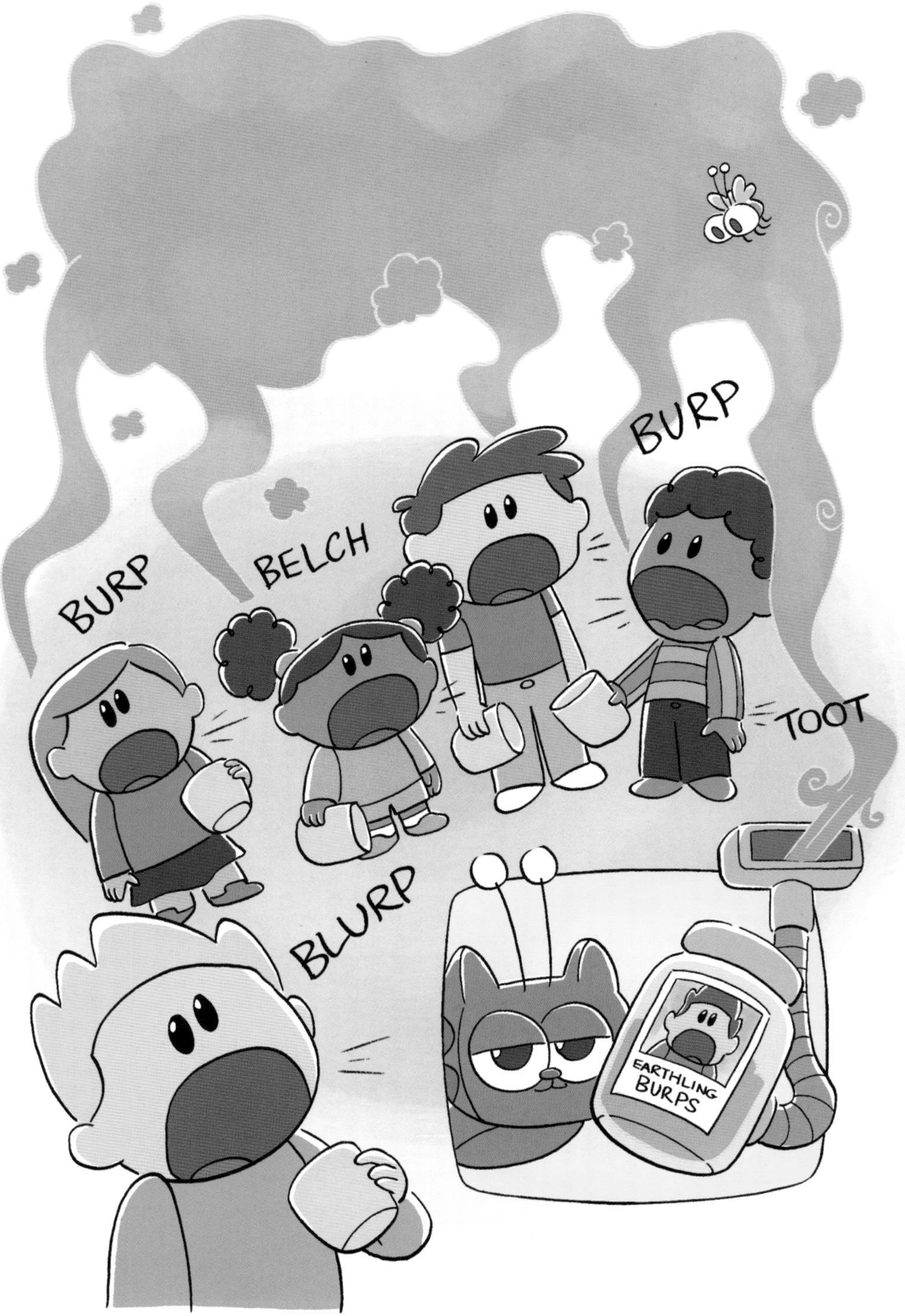
BURP
BELCH
BURP
TOOT
BLURP
EARTHLING BURPS

Chapter 8
Suck In the Skunk Spray!

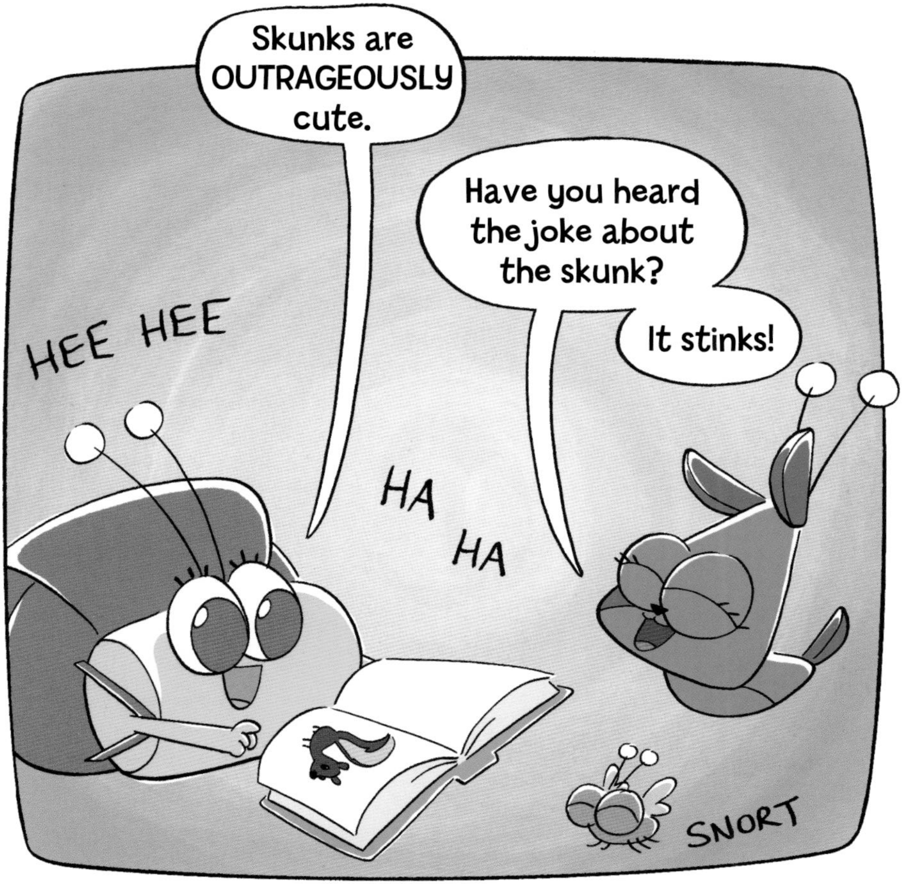
Skunks are OUTRAGEOUSLY cute.
HEE HEE
Have you heard the joke about the skunk?
It stinks!
HA HA
SNORT

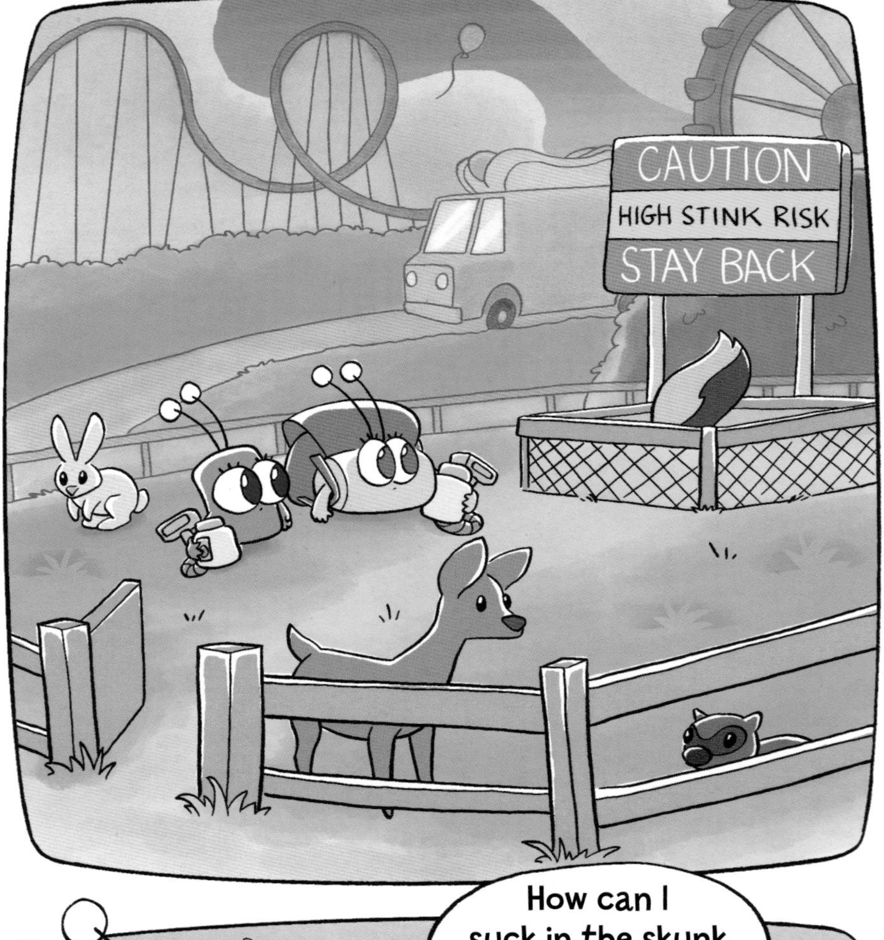
CAUTION
HIGH STINK RISK
STAY BACK

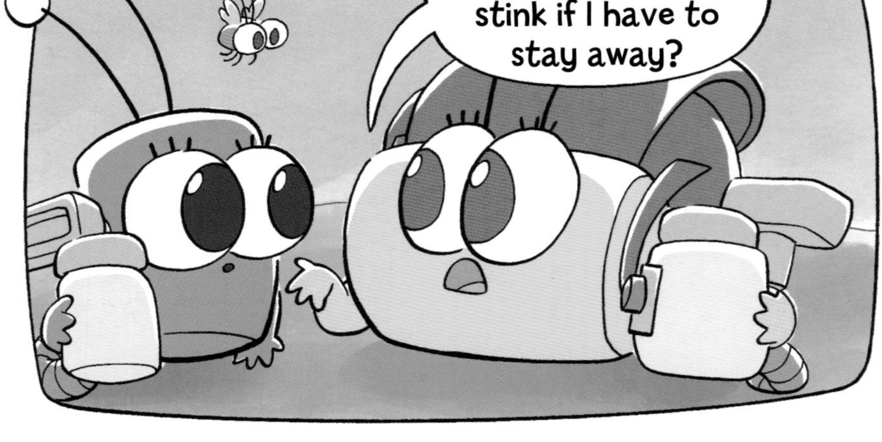
How can I suck in the skunk stink if I have to stay away?

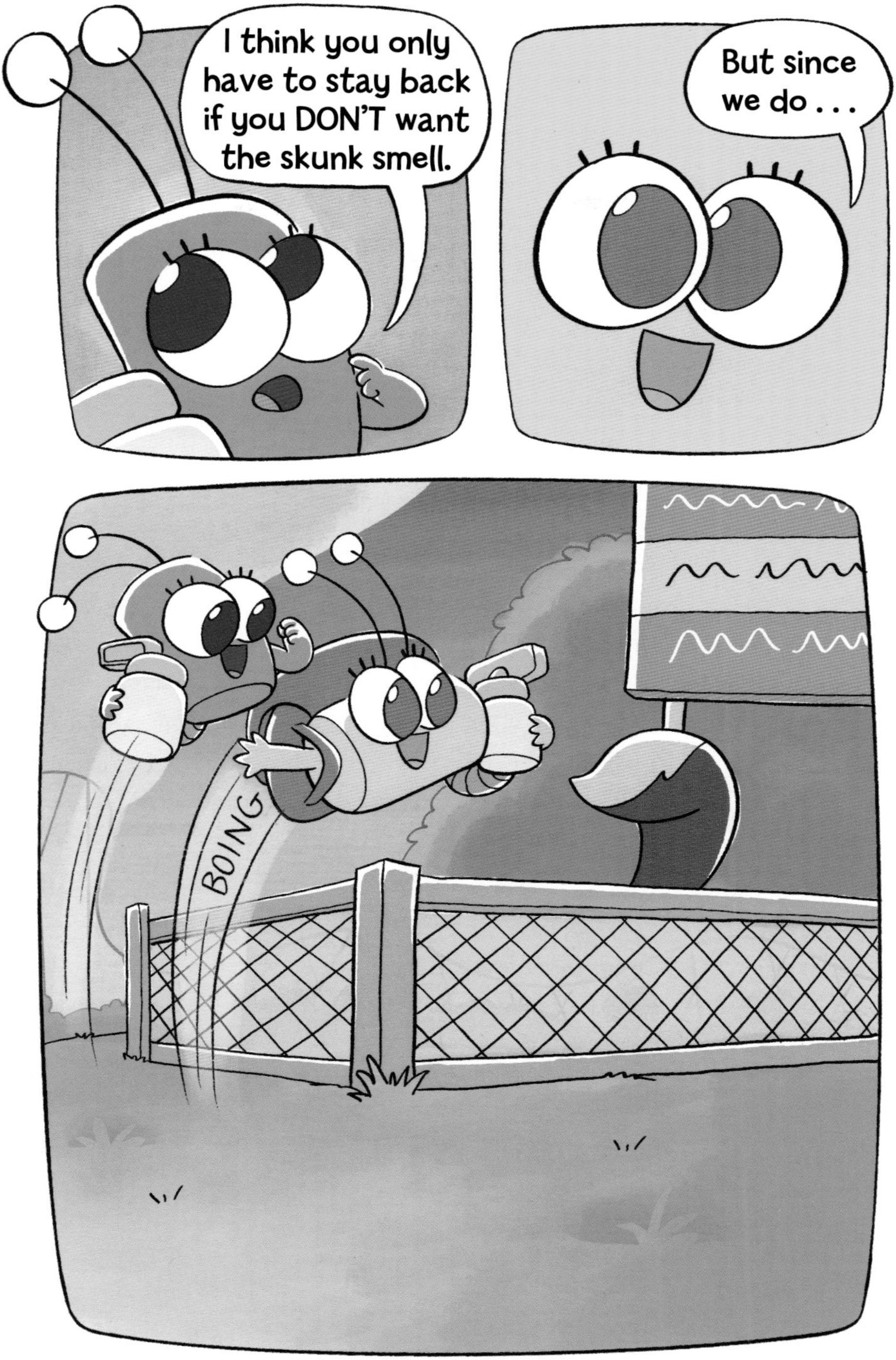
I think you only have to stay back if you DON'T want the skunk smell.
But since we do . . .
BOING

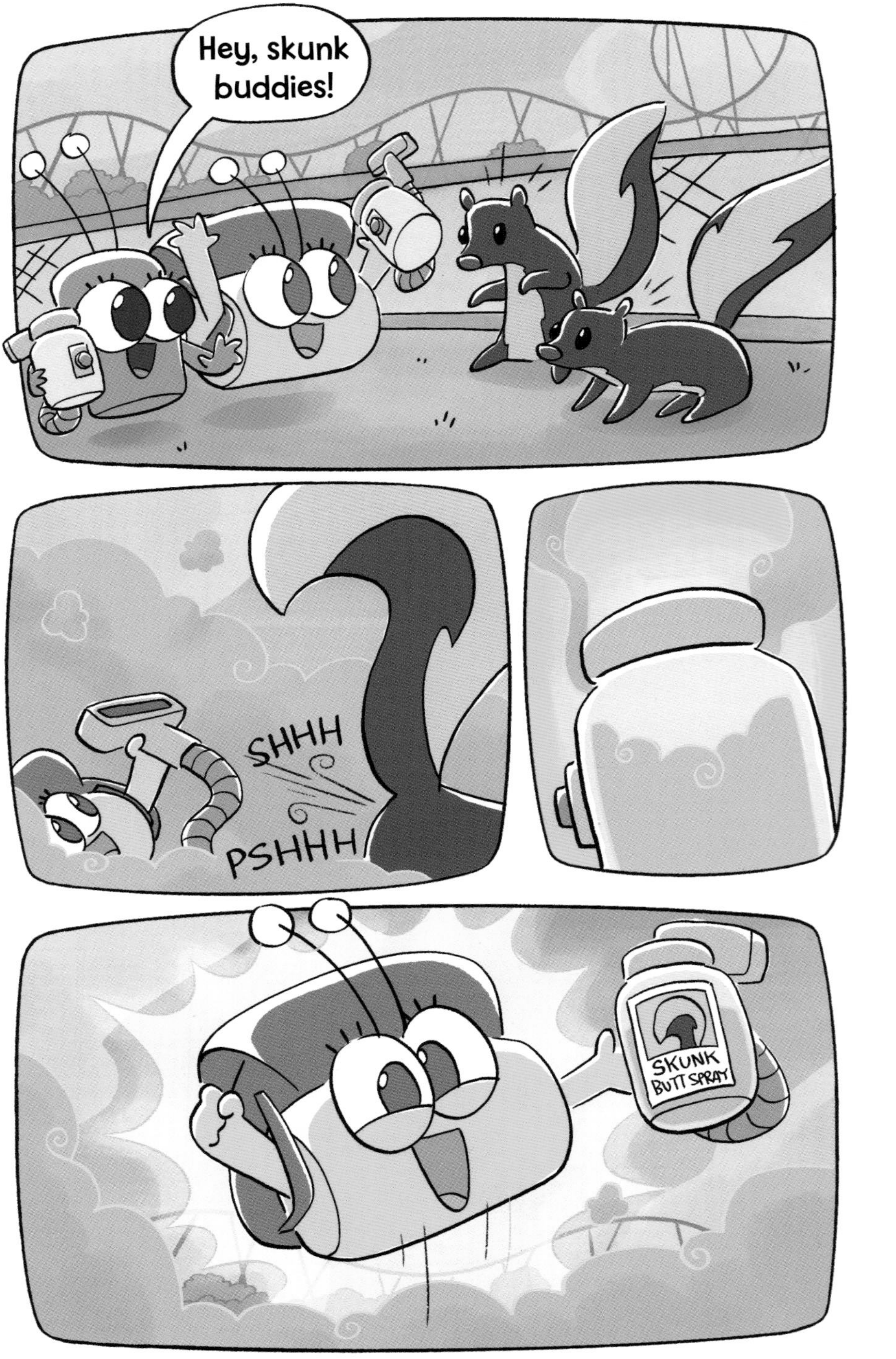
Hey, skunk buddies!
SHHH
PSHHH
SKUNK BUTT SPRAY

Chapter 9

Show and Smell Extravaganza!

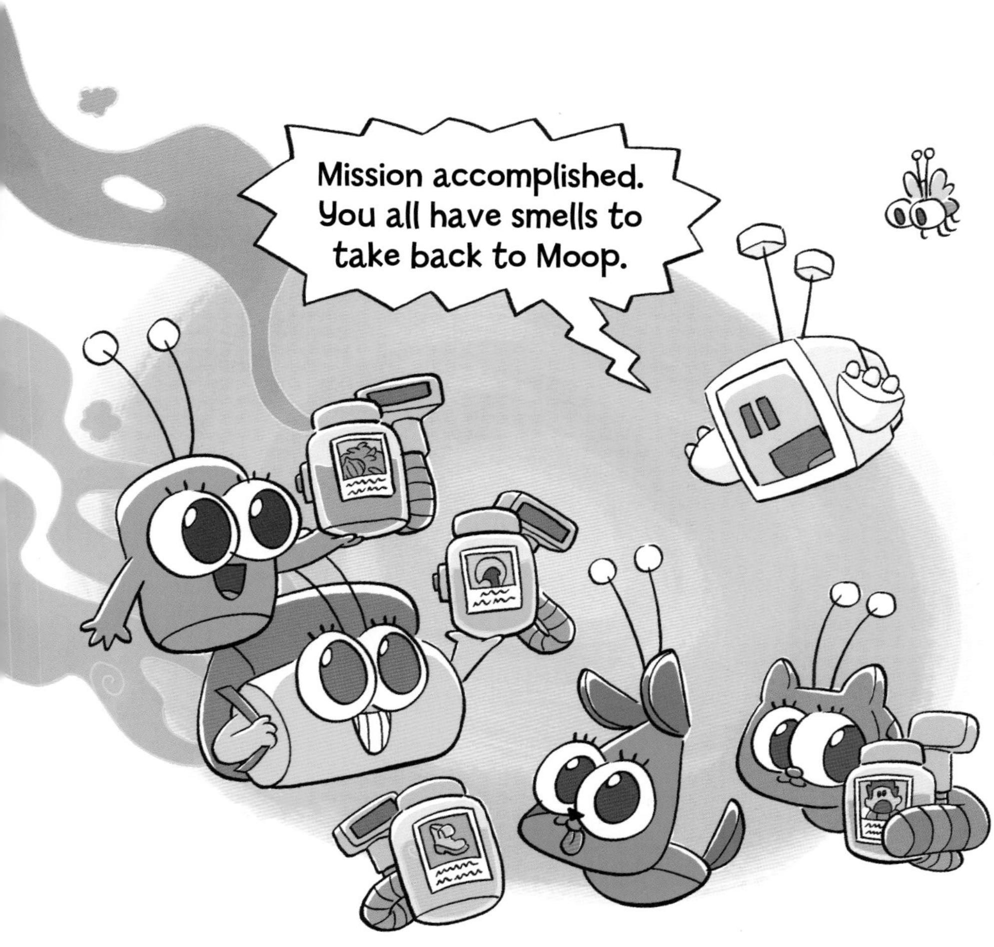
Mission accomplished. You all have smells to take back to Moop.

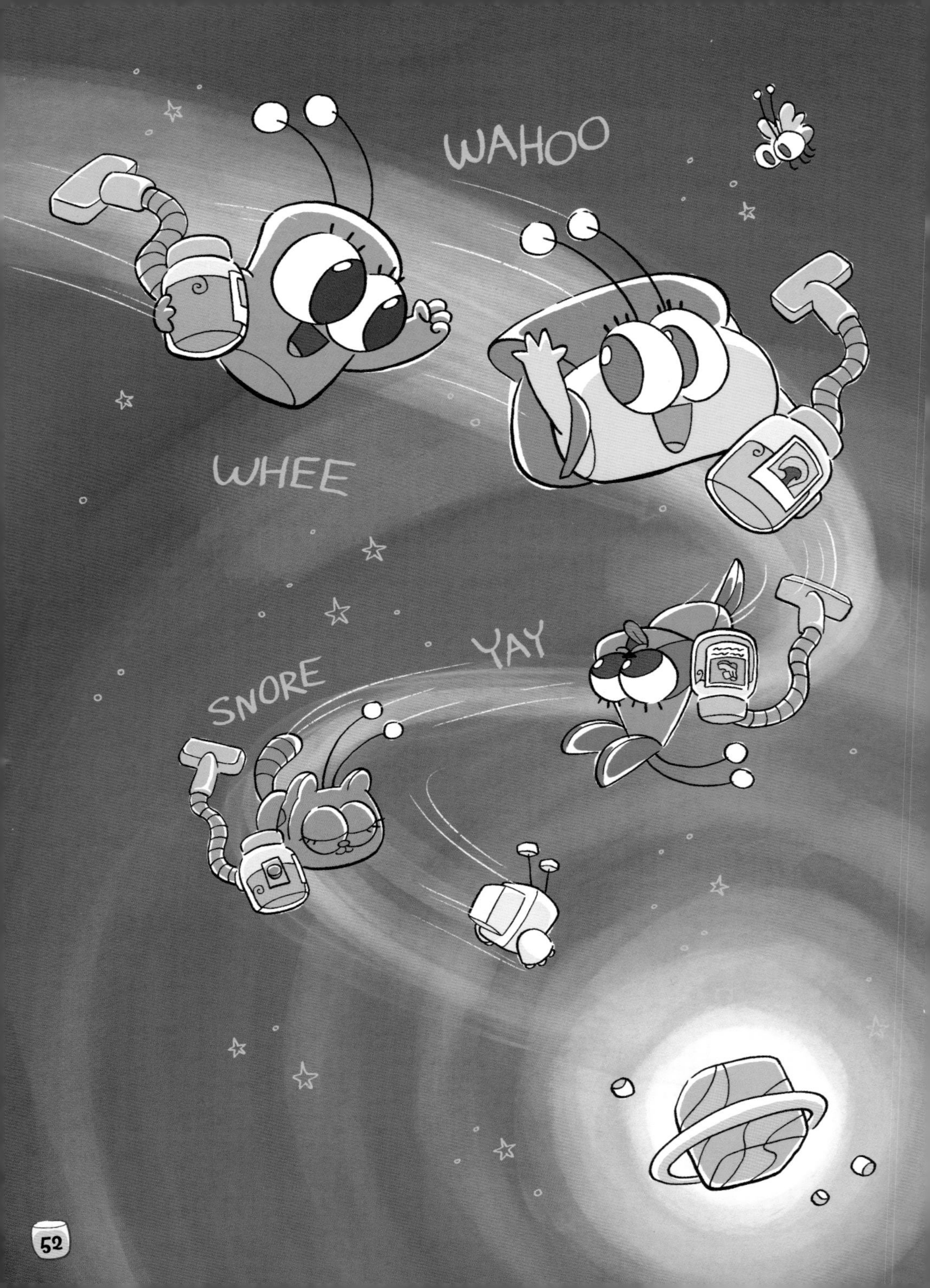
WAHOO
WHEE
YAY
SNORE

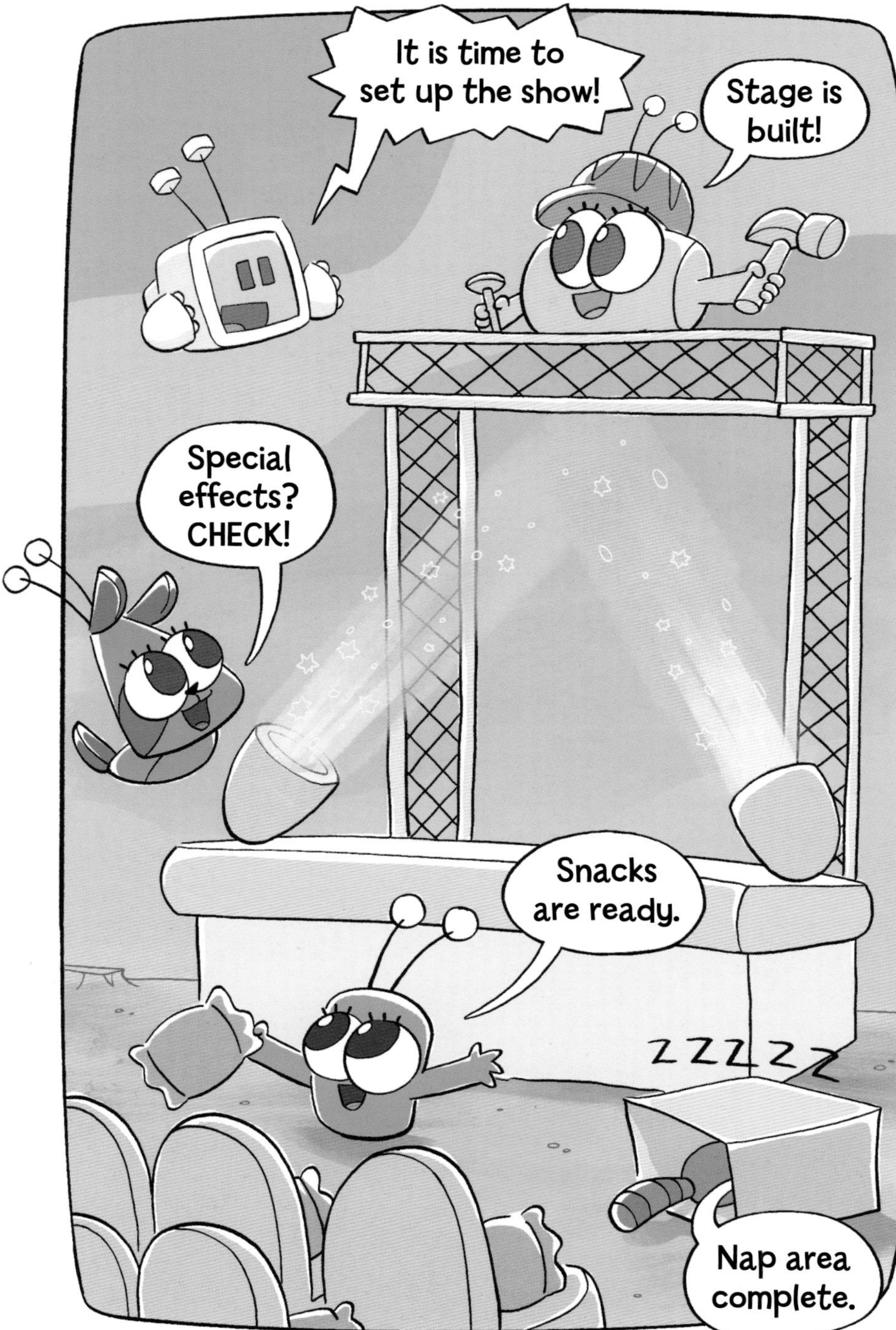
It is time to set up the show!
Stage is built!
Special effects? CHECK!
Snacks are ready.
ZZZZZ
Nap area complete.

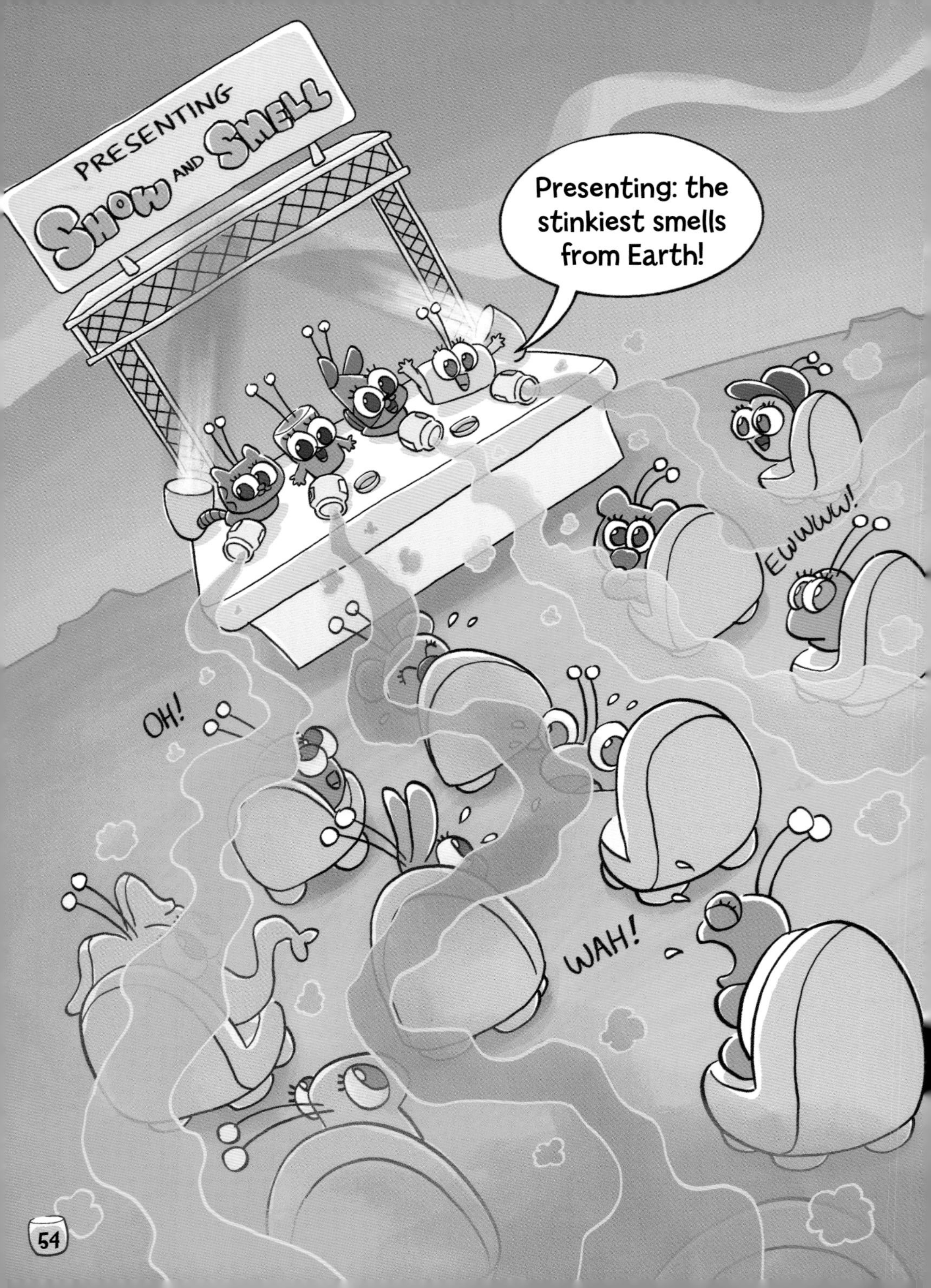
PRESENTING
SHOW AND SMELL
Presenting: the stinkiest smells from Earth!
EWWWW!
OH!
WAH!

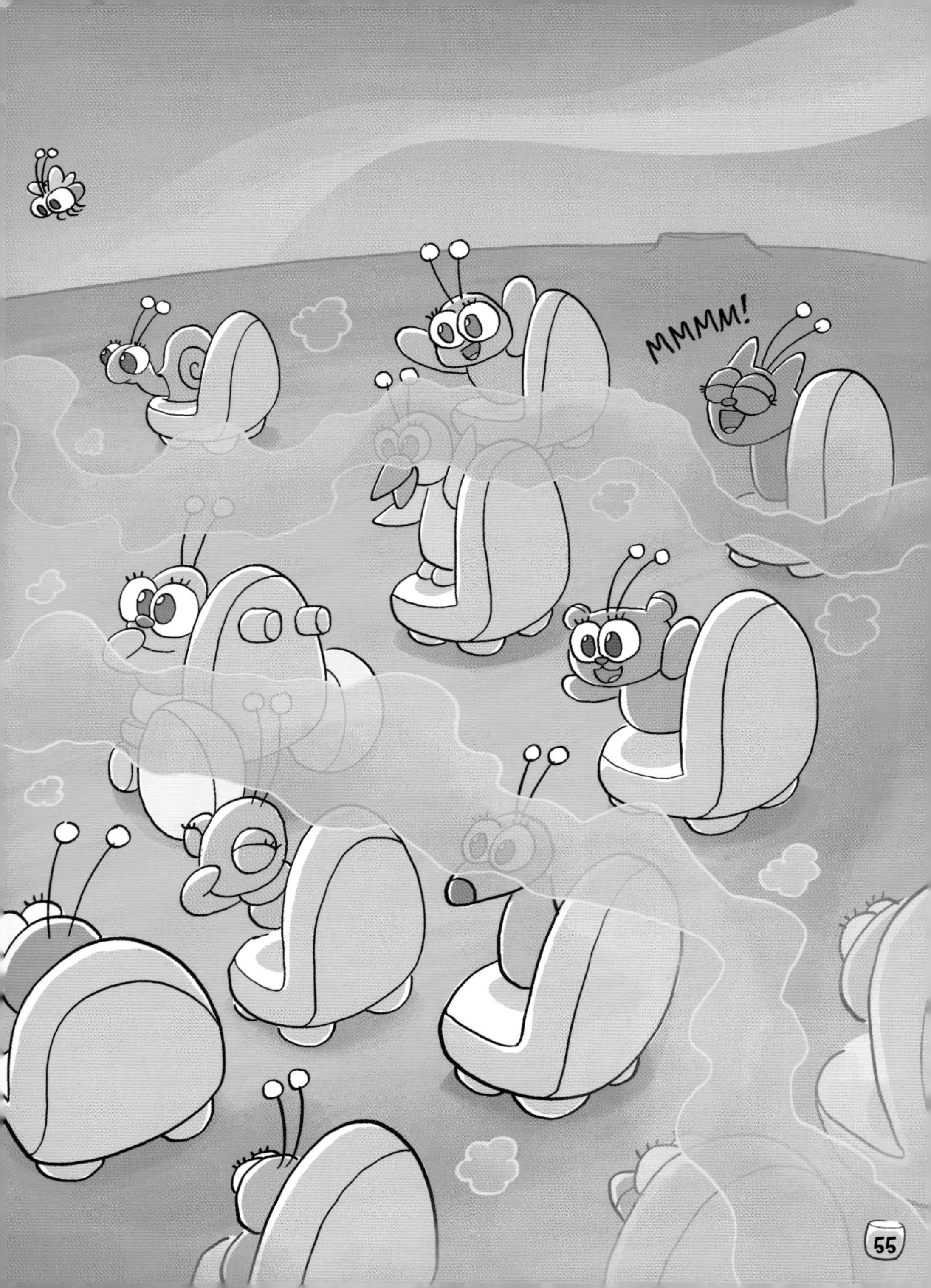
MMMM!

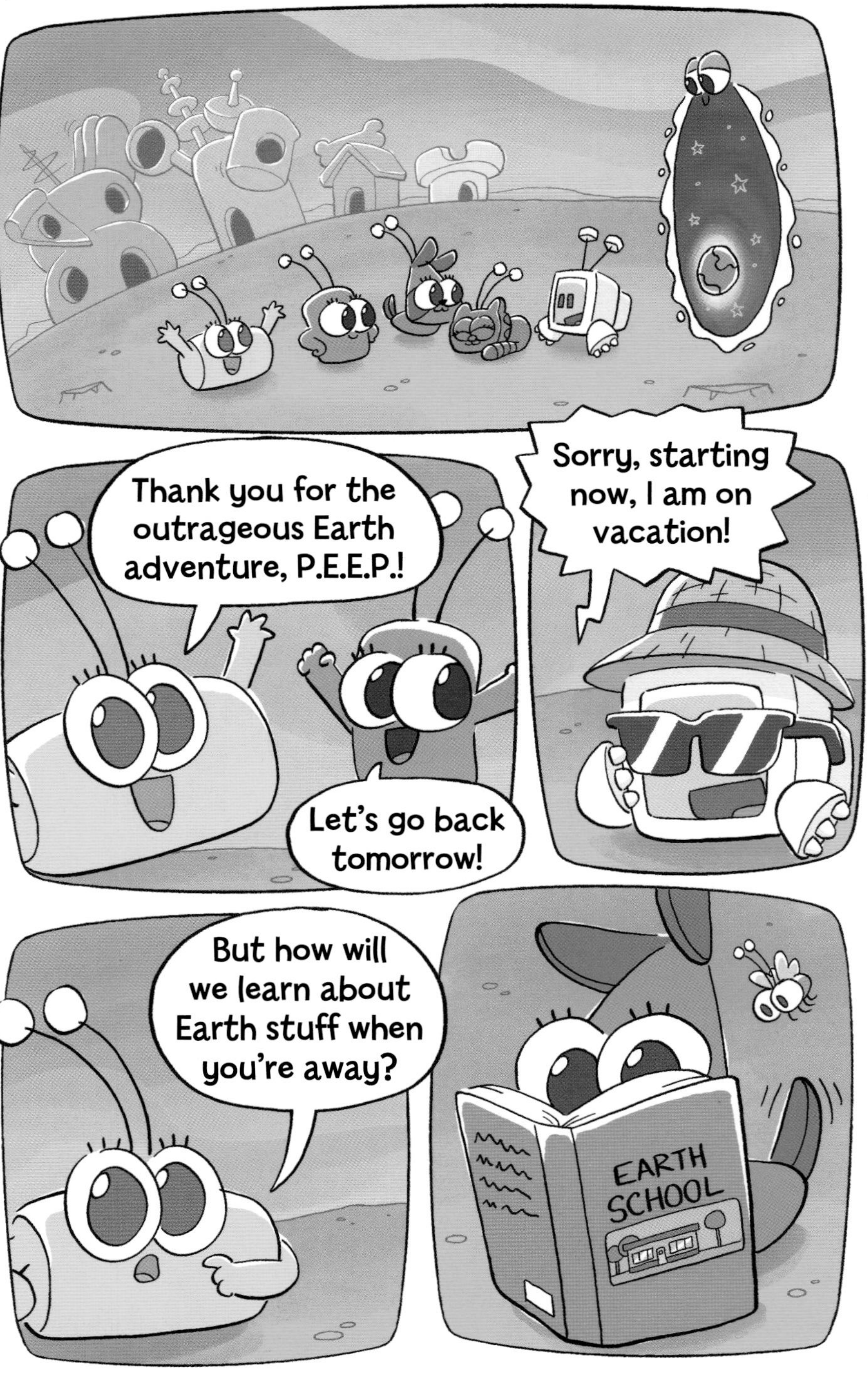
Thank you for the outrageous Earth adventure, P.E.E.P.!
Let's go back tomorrow!
Sorry, starting now, I am on vacation!
But how will we learn about Earth stuff when you're away?
EARTH SCHOOL

Acknowledgments

Squooshy thanks to all the people making the MMs come to life, especially Gemma Cooper, Heidi Kilgras, Jan Gerardi, and Michelle Cunningham. #teamworkmakesthedreamwork

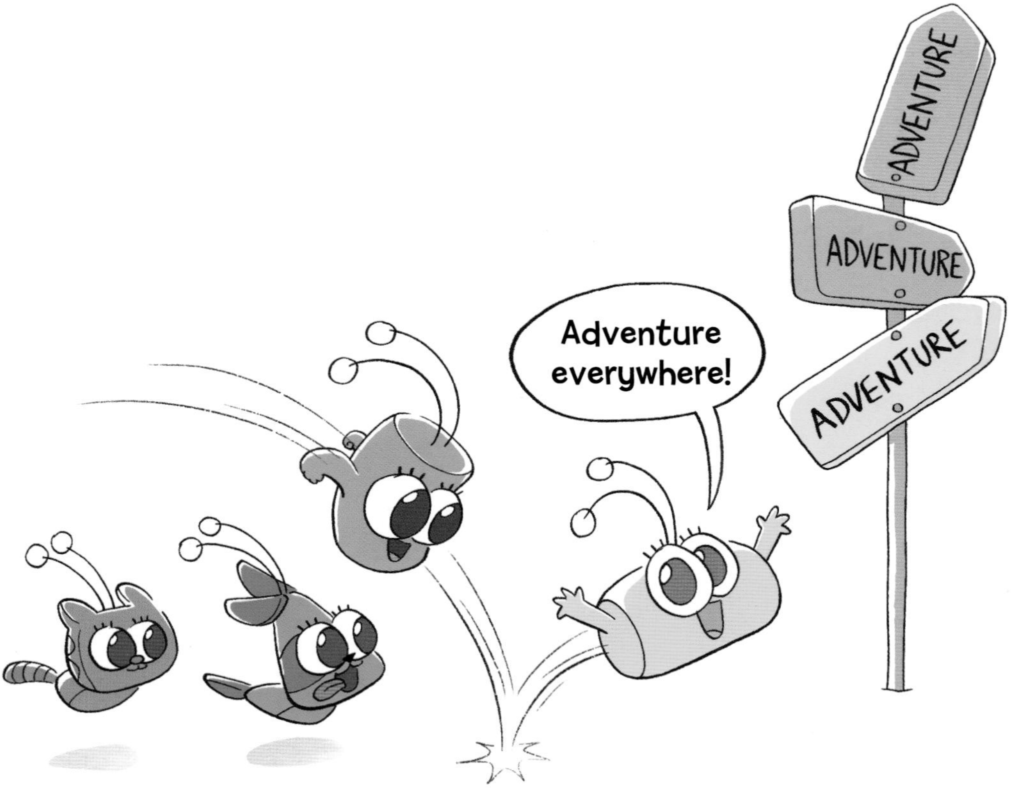
Adventure everywhere!
ADVENTURE
ADVENTURE
ADVENTURE

How to Draw Snug!

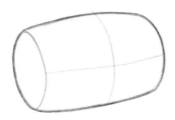

1. Start with a long, squishy marshmallow shape.

2. Draw Snug's eyes, arms, and mouth!

3. Add antennae, a tongue, and eye shines.

4. Erase any extra lines, and add color!

Note from Neil: If your drawing of Snug looks different from the Snug in this book, that's amazing! It means you've added your own artistic flair and made it one of a kind. It's fun to make characters.

Deanna Kent and **Neil Hooson** are a writer-artist duo in Kelowna, Canada. Deanna loves twinkle lights, Edna Mode, and hiking in the Great Bear Rainforest, where she's obsessed with taking photos of mushrooms, slugs, and other foresty things. Neil is king of his Les Paul guitar, makes killer enchiladas, and dreams of seeing the pyramids one day. He really wants aliens to land in his backyard. By far, their greatest creative challenge is raising four (very busy, very amazing) boys and their giant dog, Hugo.

Visit them on the web at deannaandneil.com.

🐦 @DeannaandNeil

Lunch boxes, recess, and gym—oh my! The Marshmallow Martians are about to get SCHOOLED!!

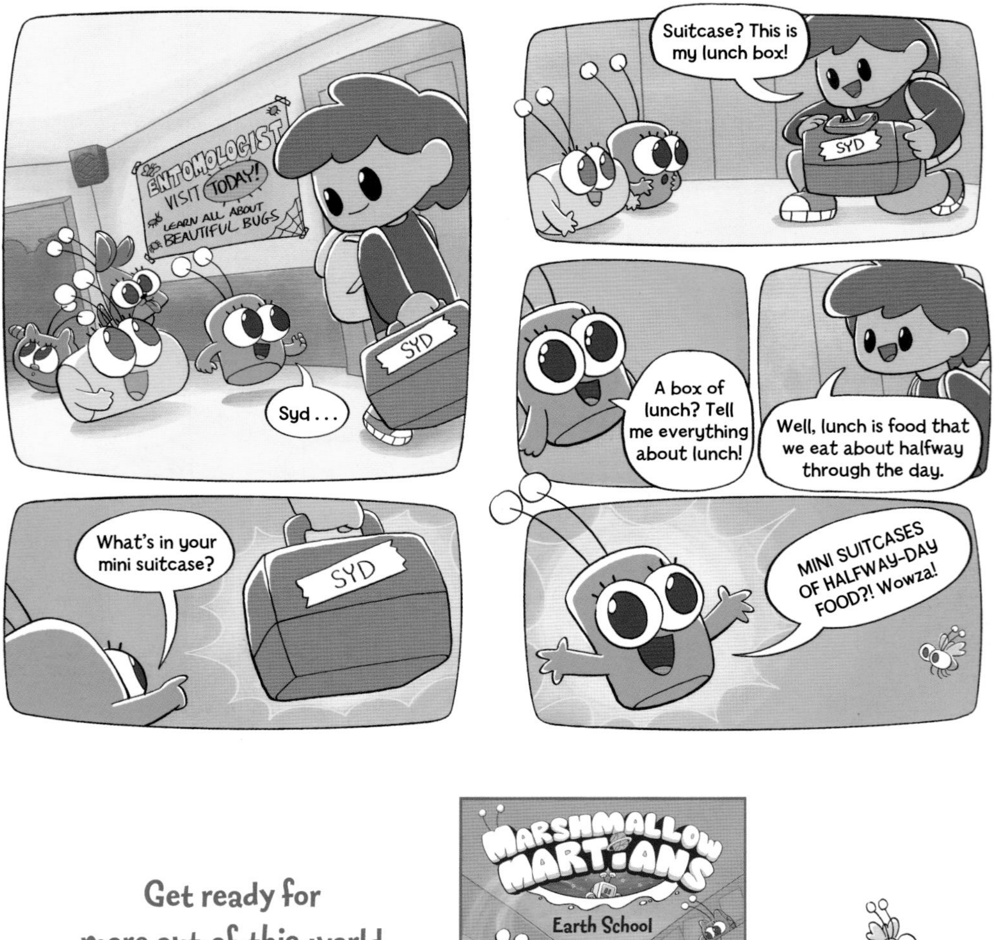
ENTOMOLOGIST
VISIT TODAY!
LEARN ALL ABOUT
BEAUTIFUL BUGS
SYD
Syd . . .
Suitcase? This is my lunch box!
SYD
A box of lunch? Tell me everything about lunch!
Well, lunch is food that we eat about halfway through the day.
What's in your mini suitcase?
SYD
MINI SUITCASES OF HALFWAY-DAY FOOD?! Wowza!

Get ready for more out-of-this-world adventures!
(Coming in summer 2023)

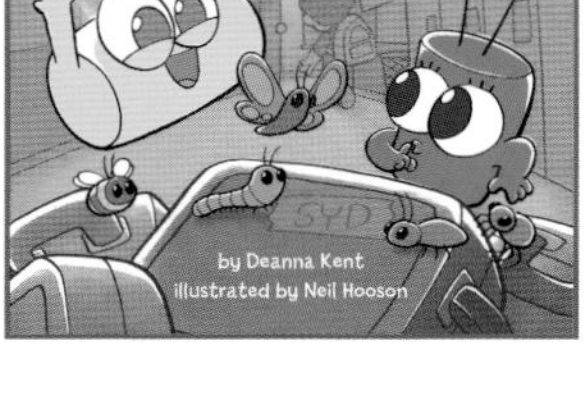
MARSHMALLOW MARTIANS
Earth School
SYD
by Deanna Kent
illustrated by Neil Hooson

AWESOME COMICS!
AWESOME KIDS!

Pizza and Taco
WHO'S THE BEST?
STEPHEN SHASKAN

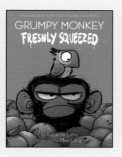

GRUMPY MONKEY
FRESHLY SQUEEZED
by Suzanne Lang
Illustrated by Max Lang

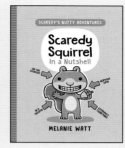

SCAREDY'S NUTTY ADVENTURES
Scaredy Squirrel
In a Nutshell
MELANIE WATT

PAULINA GANUCHEAU
LEMON BIRD
Can Help!

MARY POPE OSBORNE'S
MAGIC TREE HOUSE
THE GRAPHIC NOVEL
DINOSAURS BEFORE DARK
ADAPTED BY JENNY LAIRD
ILLUSTRATED BY KELLY & NICOLE MATTHEWS

SHARK AND BOT
Brian Yanish

BOBO and PUP-PUP
LET'S MAKE CAKE!
Vikram Madan • Nicola Slater

SUPER PANCAKE
by MEGAN WAGNER LLOYD
ABHI ALWAR

MARSHMALLOW MARTIANS
Show and Smell
by Deanna Kent
illustrated by Neil Hooson

Introduce your youngest reader to comics with

RH GRAPHIC

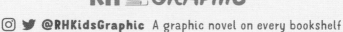

[Instagram] [Twitter] **@RHKidsGraphic** A graphic novel on every bookshelf

RHCB

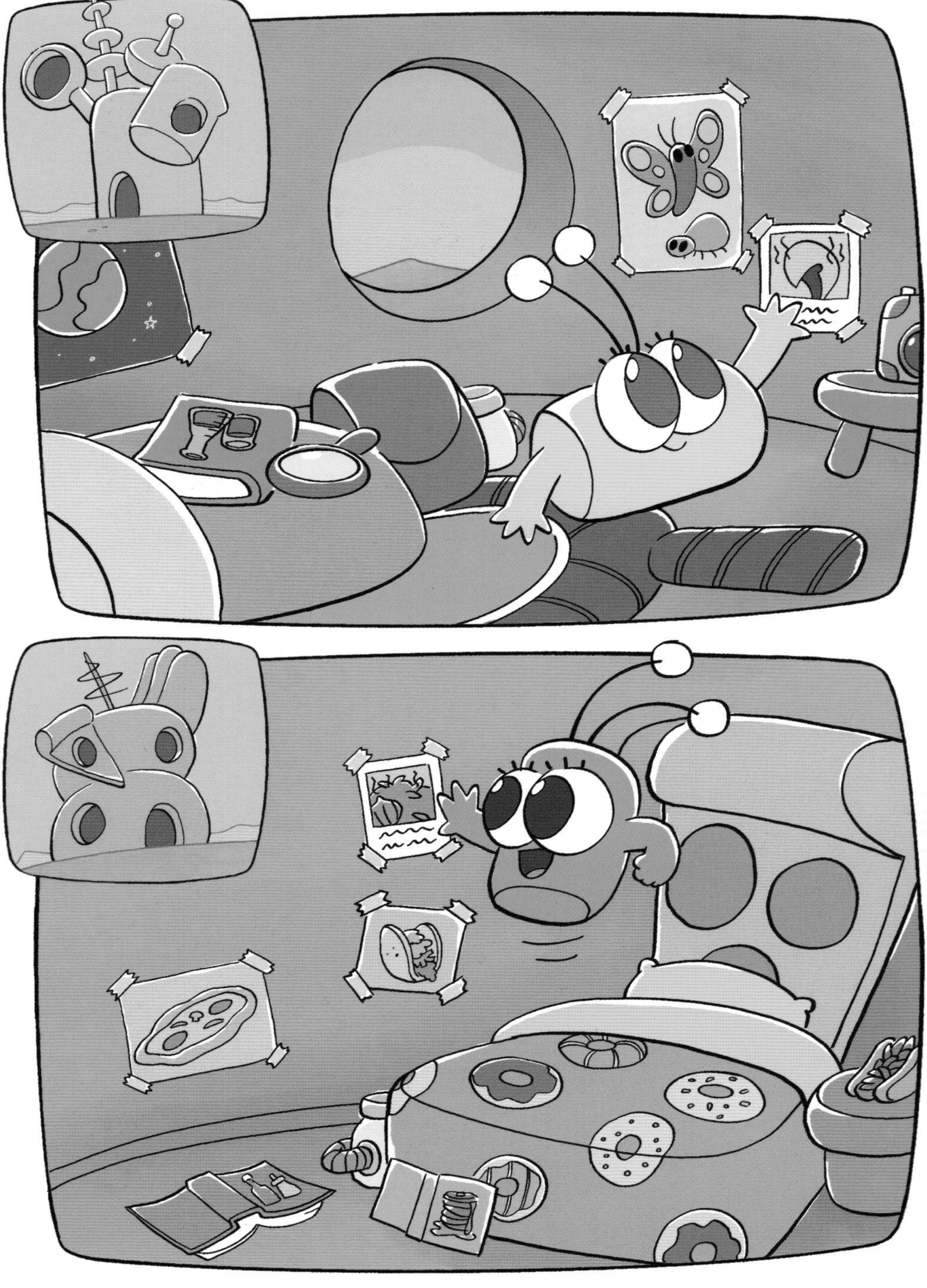